DEAL WITH THE DEVIL
BOOK ONE

The Devil's Bargain

CARIN HART

Copyright © 2023 by Carin Hart

All rights reserved.

No part of this book may be reproduced in any form or by any electronic or mechanical means, including information storage and retrieval systems, without written permission from the author, except for the use of brief quotations in a book review.

Cover by JoY Design Studio

Images of Ava & Lincoln from Adobe Stock

For those who love the idea of a powerful, morally grey bastard who is so obsessed with you, he'll spend fifteen years waiting for his second chance...

...and then he takes it—and you.

FOREWORD

Thank you for checking out *The Devil's Bargain*!

This book is a dark romance standalone featuring the organized crime leader first mentioned in *No One Has To Know*, Lincoln "Devil" Crewes, and the woman he's spent fifteen years obsessing over. It is a standalone with explicit, open door scenes, a HEA at the end, and it introduces readers to the seedy side of Springfield, a fictional town that could be anywhere in the United States, with a dynamic that is all too real today.

If you've read the interconnected standalone that is part of this same series, you'll have an idea of the level of darkness in this romance. The hero has wanted the heroine for years, and he takes his chance as soon as he can. He's still a dark-haired, morally grey man who will kill anyone for looking at his Ava wrong, but his dedication to her is never in doubt (to the readers, of

FOREWORD

course, who can get in Link's head — when it comes to Ava, it's harder to understand his motives... though she will by the end). There is no cheating or OWD/OMD in this book, but I do want readers to be aware of all other content warnings so that they can read responsibly.

The Devil's Bargain includes: murder (on and off-page), blackmail/forced marriage, dub-con/CNC, somnophilia (and cockwarming), public sex acts performed on the FMC without explicit consent, threats of rape and attempted SA (not by the MMC), religious imagery, guns, mentions of sex work (at the hero's club), drugging, kidnapping, and mentions of past stalking by the hero.

If that's something you feel comfortable reading, please enjoy!

xoxo,
Carin

the life

Mrs. Crewes

ONE
JOEY

AVA

I always remember to lock my front door when I'm home alone. But tonight? It must have slipped my mind.

How else could my ex have let himself in while I was busy in the kitchen, putting my dinner dishes away before I went up to bed?

I wasn't with Joey Maglione long enough to get to the "exchanging house keys" stage of the relationship, let alone moving him into my home. I never even visited his place, and considering our three-month relationship consisted of dinner dates and that was about all before it fizzled out toward the end of the school year, he'd barely been to mine.

But there he is. Sitting on my couch, legs spread, arms crossed over his chest, he's staring at the swinging door that separates my kitchen from my living room as though he's been waiting all night for me to notice him.

I'm used to seeing him in casual wear. Polos. Button-downs. Khakis or pressed pants. He told me he worked in sales; he definitely dressed like he did whenever I saw him. His tight black t-shirt, dark denim jeans, and construction worker boots aren't what I'm used to, but I know that handsome face with his steely blue eyes and sandy brown hair.

The smirk, though? That's new, and I stop a few steps past the threshold.

The door swings into my back. I barely notice.

"Joey? What—"

That's as far as I get before I notice the gun perched on his thigh and my sentence—my heart, too, for the most part—stops short.

Gun? I don't know what Joey's doing in my living room, but I'm even more clueless when it comes to why he would have brought a *gun* here with him.

My eyes fly up to his face. His smirk widens. He knows I saw his gun—and, for some reason, that amuses him.

"Hey, Ava, baby. Good to see you again."

I pointedly refuse to acknowledge his weapon, almost as though I could make it disappear by pretending it's not there. "What are you doing here? It's late."

It's almost eleven o'clock at night. Normally, I'm in

bed before ten. I have to be up early to get ready for school, but we've been out for two weeks now. My schedule gets a little thrown off during summer break, though I'm still an early-to-bed, early-to-rise kind of girl whether it's September or July.

Joey knows that. It's one of those little things that kept on adding up until we both had to admit that we were incompatible. Despite being in his mid-thirties like me, he enjoyed the nightlife while I've never been a fan. He had to have thought I was sleeping even as he's wide awake. Yet he's here—he's here with a *gun*—and I have no idea why.

I continue to try to ignore his weapon. That's impossible when he snatches it up, holding it easily in his hand as he gets to his feet.

"Oh, I know it's late. Saint Ava... just can't stomach the idea of having a man in your house after dark, huh?"

It's the tone of voice that catches my attention first. I remember Joey as having a kind yet undeniably suave manner of speaking. A gentleman. He always respected my pace, never pushing me for more than I was willing to give, and was sweet about it.

Not now.

He has a dark edge to his words, part sneer, part scoff that's only highlighted by the way he looks me up and down.

I'm in my nightclothes: an oversized t-shirt, no bra, and a pair of sleep shorts. I'd changed earlier while I was snuggled up with a blanket on the couch, watching some mindless television. When I was ready for bed, I turned off the TV, went and put away my dishes from dinner, and was just about to head for my room when I found Joey waiting for me.

His lip curls when he sees the outline of my boobs against the thin fabric. My nipples are poking through, courtesy of my air conditioner being on full blast, and he can't take his eyes off of them.

Me? I'm staring back at him, too.

Because while his tone might have caught my attention at first, it's not the only thing that did.

"What did you call me?"

Saint Ava... long before Link left me for a life of crime, I was always the goodie-goodie to his bad boy rep. Only we knew the truth about who the other really was, and while those school-age teases proved pretty apt as we grew up and went from lovey-dovey teens to life-hardened adults—Link, with his criminal empire, and me, teaching first-graders at Springfield Elementary—when my first boyfriend called me 'Saint Ava', it was his pet name for me.

My ex says it like it's a curse... but he shouldn't know that nickname at all.

I wait. Joey doesn't answer me, though his smirk develops a cruel edge as his expression darkens.

My stomach twists. Oh, I don't like this. I don't like this one bit.

I cross my arm over my chest, hiding my boobs. "I think you should go."

"Go? So soon? Oh, Ava, baby, I don't think so. That's not gonna happen. At least, I'm not leaving on my own." Lifting his gun, he aims it dead at my covered chest as he takes a few pointed steps toward me. "When I finally leave here tonight, you'll be coming with me."

Looking down the barrel of his gun, I go absolutely still.

When he grabs his dick through his jeans with his free hand, I start to tremble.

His smirk gets impossibly wider.

"Way I see it," Joey adds, "there's no rush. Gus said I gotta bring you to the boss. You just have to be breathing, he told me. He didn't say a damn thing about me taking my cut a little early."

My mind is spinning even as I don't move a muscle.

Who's Gus? Boss? What boss? I don't know who Joey made sales for, but I can't imagine his employers wanting anything to do with me.

I finally swallow, then find my voice again. "Your cut?"

"Don't be coy, Ava. You're cute, but not when you're playing dumb like this."

I wish I was playing.

One hand still on his crotch, Joey wags the gun at me. "You owe me. You know you do."

I'm so confused. The gun's not making it any easier for me to think, either.

"Owe you *what*?"

"You never let me fuck you. You ate the food I bought, and sat next to me in my ride, but, oh, your precious pussy was too good for me. Was that it? You fuck Sinners, but the rest of us are trash compared to those assholes. Huh?"

Sinners.

Link.

Fifteen years. It's been fifteen years since he walked out on me, and now Joey's throwing Link's old name for me in my face *and* the gang he traded me in for.

What the hell is going on? I don't understand. Forget Link for a second; impossible, yeah, since I've never been able to. Joey... the man glaring at me from behind his weapon looks like the sweet Joey I knew, but he's certainly not acting like him.

You never let me fuck you...

When I explained to him that I didn't have sex with any of my dates until I felt comfortable with them, he told me he agreed. That he didn't mind waiting.

My mouth is suddenly dry. I swallow again, trying to bring some moisture back before I say in a voice full of false bravado, "I don't know what you think you're doing, but this has gone on long enough. I want you to leave."

Despite the fear rushing through me, I thought I

sounded pretty firm. Maybe I did, but Joey just proves how much I don't know him at all when he makes his move, crossing the distance between us before I can react.

He's too quick. Breaking for me, he's inches away right as I open my mouth to scream for help.

"Saint Ava," he sneers, collaring my throat with one strong hand, crudely squeezing my tit with the other as he mashes the handle of the gun against it. "The virgin who *isn't*."

I thrash against his hold. "Let go of me!"

Joey shifts his grip. He twists my nipple before reaching up with his free hand to dig his fingers into my cheeks when I do actually get to scream. Using his palm to jam my jaw shut, my shouts are cut off as he forces me to just about choke on my tongue.

Moving me again, Joey closes the small gap between us. His hot breath on the shell of my ear has me whimpering through my clenched teeth as he pants, "When Damien gets his hands on you, you'll be glad to have something to look back on. Because I'm not going anywhere until I get inside that cunt, baby, but once Damien has you? You'll wish it was just my dick you gotta ride… if you survive meeting the boss for the first time, that is."

Damien—

Damien.

Even in my panicked brain, I know who he means: Damien Libellula. A name only ever spoken of in whispers, but one that nearly everyone in town knows because it's dangerous *not* to.

In Springfield, there are two rival organized crime rings: Damien Libellula's mob-run 'Family' set on the East End of the city, and the Sinners Syndicate, ruled by an enigmatic figure known only as Devil—but who I still think of as Link.

If Joey came to my house tonight on Damien's orders, he must work for the Libellula Family. I haven't had any contact with Link for years, so I know I couldn't have been targeted by the mafia because of my former relationship with him, but somehow I have regardless of why.

And if I can't get away from my most recent ex, he has every intention of fucking me, then turning me over to Damien Libellula, the second most dangerous man in Springfield. Both are awful fates, but put together?

He's right. I *won't* survive.

I have to get away from him. That's all I'm thinking about. Get away, get some help, and then get the hell out of Springfield. My whole life is here—my job and my friends, and my parents' graves, too—but if the Libellula Family has put a target on my back, I have to run before one of his men hits a bullseye.

I never get the chance. Before I can tap into my adrenaline and fight for my escape, Joey shoves me away from him, hooking his boot behind my bare foot.

I trip backward, landing roughly on my ass as I hit the floor.

As he looms over me, his expression goes dark.

Paralyzed like a whimpering prey staring up at the big, bad predator, I can't move.

With a flick of his finger, Joey unbuttons his jeans. "Make it good for me, baby, and maybe I'll stand up for you with the boss. Instead of being Family puss, I'll see if you can be only mine."

That breaks me free of my paralysis. I never want to see Joey Maglione again, let alone feel his hands on me.

I'm not so sure I'll be able to avoid that tonight—but I'm going to try.

Shaking my head, I start to yell as loudly as I can.

"Help—"

He's on top of me before I can finish my shout.

the life

Mrs. Crewes

TWO
DEAD

AVA

Once Joey has my writhing body on my back, he shoves his knees between my legs, keeping me from closing them to him completely.

Before I can go for his face and claw his eyes out—do something, *anything*—he drops his gun next to him and takes my wrists in an iron-tight hold. His weight presses down on me, trapping me on the carpet as he shifts my hands, taking both of mine in one of his.

Now that he has a free hand again, he jams it up my shorts, fingers stabbing into my pussy. One of them finds my entrance, penetrating me while I shriek.

Still screaming as loud as I can, hoping one of my neighbors will hear me, I wiggle beneath him, trying to break out of his hold and get his damn finger out of me.

Joey digs his elbow into my gut to kill my scream *and* keep me from wriggling away from him. As I gasp, choking on both the fear and the pain, he lets go of his grip on me before leaning back on his heels, tugging on his zipper with the hand that was just up my shorts. The zipper catches on the material of his boxers. For a heartbeat, he's distracted, trying to get his pants off, and he lets go of my hands so that he can fix the zipper.

I guess he thought I was resigned to my fate when I stopped screaming. Yeah, right. The second he lets go of me, I see my chance. Bracing myself on my hands, I scoot far enough away from him that I can rear back my leg, then kick him right in the dick with the heel of my foot.

Joey howls as I connect. The shock of the pain has him falling to his side, curled up in the fetal position as he realizes I basically just tried to mule-kick his erection off of him.

I scamper to my feet, purposely kicking his gun away while praying to God I don't blow off my bare toes. They hurt like hell as they hit the hard handle, but as the stupid thing skips away, it doesn't go off.

My insane ex certainly does.

"You fucking bitch," he snarls when he gets his breath back, cupping his groin with one hand. His other beats against my floor, eyes blazing with hatred as he watches me try to desperately put some distance between us. "I'll make you pay for that!"

He can't kill me. Right? He's supposed to bring me to his boss. Breathing, he said. That has to mean alive. He can't *kill* me—

Joey climbs up to one knee, hand slapping the ground, searching for his gun. It didn't get too far, only about three feet across my living room, and he sees it once he takes his eyes off of me.

He's quick. Terrified for my life, I'm *quicker*.

Next to my couch, there's an end table with a side drawer. Racing for it, I have it open, pistol in hand before he's halfway to his gun.

"Hey, asshole."

His head shoots up. Still hunched over in agony, a low chuckle manages to escape him when he sees what I'm holding.

"Please, Ava," Joey scoffs, his voice raw from his howl. "You can't honestly think I believe you know how to handle one of those."

He's right. I have no idea what I'm doing past what I looked up on Google when the gun first showed up at my house.

It was five years ago, back when I finally traded my last apartment for a house of my own. About a week after I finished unpacking, an unmarked brown box showed up in my mailbox. The gun was inside. With it, a white card that had a single minimalist drawing of a devil on it: red horns and a pointed tail curved beneath it.

Link sent it to me. I hadn't spoken to him since I was twenty-two and saw him staring at me from across the midway at the Springfield Mall. All the same hurt, rejection, pain, and love hit me then, and I called him, begging him for closure, even though he walked out on me two years prior. He hadn't been able to explain himself anymore then than he had when he first left—just telling me that he'd come back for me when he was "worthy"—and I'd... I'd given up.

I'd moved on.

And then, eight years later, the Devil of Springfield sent me a handgun when I lived on my own without neighbors in spitting distance for the very first time.

For protection? I'd decided it was and, after researching the make and model of the gun he sent, I shoved it in my side drawer before trying my best to forget about it.

It's loaded. With a determined flick of my fingernail, I disengage the safety. My Colt Mustang is a pocket pistol, barely a pound, and I lift it up so that Joey can't miss it.

"Leave." My voice is as shaky as my hands. "Get the fuck out of my house."

"You want me to go, baby? You'll have to shoot me first."

I will. If that's what I have to do, I *will*. "Just go."

He doesn't.

Instead, pushing off of the ground, he launches himself at me.

The last glimpse I get of Joey Maglione is his handsome face twisted in a vicious sneer and I know instantly that, if I let him get his hands on me again, he won't be satisfied with just fucking me because I never let him before. If he reaches me, I'm dead.

I'm fucking *dead*.

So I can't let him get his hands on me, can I?

Closing my eyes, praying again to whoever will listen that I don't miss, I squeeze the trigger.

Shooting a gun in real life is nothing like what you see on television and in the movies. I have my Colt positioned between both of my hands as it spits out the bullet. The only reason I don't slice my palms open when the barrel slide recoils is because I'm so terrified of the thing that my grip isn't as tight as it could've been. My arms jerk with the recoil, though, and the explosion of the actual shot has my ears ringing.

I'm not expecting the smoke that floods my face. It stinks like rotten eggs, making me choke and cough on it. My arms don't just ache, either; they tingle from the vibrations. I can feel myself gagging, though it takes a few seconds before I can hear it, too.

And that's when I realize that that's *all* I can hear.

"Joey?" I drop my arms. "Joey?"

No answer. Not a curse, not a sneer, not even his yowl of pain.

It's quiet and, for a few seconds more, I stay in the darkness before I finally open my eyes.

I immediately wish that I hadn't.

My stomach turns, from the sight and the smell, and I just manage to take a few frantic steps away from his body before mine folds over. With my hands on my knees, Link's gun still tight in my grasp, I throw up all over the floor.

Because I didn't miss, did I? With Joey so close, I didn't really think I would, but I wasn't trying to kill him. I just wanted to get him to back off, and if I had to shoot him to keep him from getting on top of me ever again, I would.

He's on the floor. Crumpled, half of his face blown away from the bullet's impact, I know that I won't have to worry about him touching me again. He's obviously dead—and I'm in big, big trouble.

I killed him. I killed my ex.

Groaning, heaving, eyes stinging with sudden tears, I lob the gun as far away from me as I can, tossing it lightly so that it doesn't accidentally discharge. My mouth tastes vile. I wipe at it with the back of my shaky hand, barely aware that I'm doing it.

He's dead. My ears are still ringing from the gunshot, and I know one of my neighbors had to have heard it. If they come here, if they check, they'll find what's left of Joey on my floor.

I run over to my TV. It takes me a few seconds to snatch the remote from where I left it on the coffee table. My fingers don't want to work. I'm muttering something under my breath—come on, come on, you stupid thing, he's dead, oh my God, he's *dead*—but all I can think about is getting the damn thing on.

Any channel, any streaming app, it doesn't matter, whatever it loads on is fine. I press buttons until sound comes through the speakers. Cranking the volume up to fifty, it's loud enough now that maybe—just maybe—my neighbors might think the gunshot came from my television.

Will that work? I don't know. Despite being familiar with a few players in Springfield's seedy underbelly, I'm not a criminal. I only had a gun because... because...

Link.

For fifteen years, I tried not to think about what kind of man my childhood sweetheart became. It's hard when even the sweet, innocent school teachers in Springfield can still hear rumors about how wicked Lincoln "Devil" Crewes is, but if there's one man who might know what to do with a dead body in the middle of your living room, it's my Link.

I need his help. Somehow, without ever meaning to, I found myself mixed up with the local criminals. If Damien Libellula sent Joey after me for some reason, the head of the East End crime family isn't going to be happy when he finds out that I killed him.

It was self-defense. I had to protect myself. If Joey hadn't tried to get his pants off... if he hadn't threatened to rape me... I never would have gone for the gun in my side drawer.

But even if I could claim self-defense, would Damien believe me?

Would the crooked police—who everyone in the city knows acts like a private force for the Springfield syndicates—believe me?

Wrapping my arms around my middle, trembling as I realize the answer to that, I have one more question: will *Link* believe me?

I don't know. The boy I loved when we were both twenty would have, before he broke my heart and walked away, never looking back. The thirty-five-year-old man he's become since then? I honestly can't say, but I do know that I don't have any other choice.

Damien Libellula is the second most dangerous man in Springfield.

The Devil of Springfield is the *first*.

Phone... phone... where's my—

Ah, there it is.

His number isn't in my phone. I did that on purpose. It would've been too, too easy to call him on those long, lonely nights if all I had to do was pull up his name. But, unless he changed it, I still have it memorized by heart.

No way he didn't change it, I tell myself even as I tap out the number. He had to have—but what if he didn't?

I have to try. If it's possible to reach Link, I have to *try*.

Ring.

Ring.

Ring...

I lose track of how many rings it takes before voicemail picks up. It's automated, spitting the number back at me, so I can't tell if it belongs to Link or not. I have to hope that it does and, despite the late hour, I call him again.

Before I can dial a third time, my phone rings. The screen shows the same number I just called.

I answer it on the second ring.

"Hello?" I gasp out. "Link? Is that you?"

Please, please, please...

"Yeah." The voice is gruff, deeper with age, but recognition sings within me. "It's me."

It's *him*.

the life

Mrs. Crewes

THREE
SECRET PHONE

LINCOLN

Leaning back in my booth, rapping the bottom of my empty shot glass against the tabletop, I watch my second out of the corner of my eye.

It's the smirk pulling on his too-fucking-pretty face. He's up to something, and I'm not in the mood to find out what. My single shot of whiskey hasn't done a damn thing to take the edge off today. The last thing I need tonight is any of his bullshit.

After knowing "Rolls" Royce McIntyre for these last ten years, I've gotten pretty good at telling when he's in "underboss" mode, and when he's pushing his luck and testing me.

In the whole damn world, there are only two people who can get away with that without fear that Devil will retaliate: Royce and—

Gritting my teeth, stretching my arm across the top of the leather seat behind me, I look out into the glitz and grit that highlight every inch of my playground. From the crowded dance floor in the middle to the private booths just like the one I'm sitting in with Royce, and the wraparound bar doing more business than every other joint in Springfield combined, it's a monument to everything I've accomplished in my thirty-five years—and a reminder of the price I paid to have it.

Even now, all this time later, I can hear her asking me *why*...

I need another shot. Fuck, I need *something*. The bass of the music pumping out of the nearby speakers seems to pulse in time to the throb at the back of my skull, and the button-down shirt I stretched over my chest for my dinner meeting earlier makes me feel like a stuffed sausage.

Knocking the shot glass away from me with my knuckles, I grumble under my breath and yank at the tie. Once I can breathe a little easier, I flick open the first two buttons on my shirt and exhale.

A little better, though I squint through the haze of the club, trying to fight back against my headache.

Usually, I don't mind the noise. My customers expect it, and the racket adds to the atmosphere. No one comes to the Devil's Playground for quiet contemplation. My club is about drinking yourself stupid, losing all your money at the tables near the back, and getting laid by one of the club girls upstairs if you can still afford it.

It wasn't always like this. Before I bought the place out, it used to be called Jimmy's Bar, but I changed the name shortly after I cobbled together the Sinners Syndicate. We needed a headquarters, a place to conduct business, and an establishment that would get the cash rolling in while we worked on bigger deals and better scores.

Nowadays, the Playground is the syndicate's main form of income—thanks to the gambling and the girls—and I know damn well most of the bit players in Springfield as well as some wannabes only come by because they're dying to get a glimpse of the Devil himself.

Good luck. On my better nights, I'll prowl around the floor, letting them wonder what it is about me that made me a legend in town. I'm sure they've heard the rumors. Most of the stories about me are true, and the ones that aren't probably pale in comparison to the shit I've done for the syndicate.

To see me, to look in Devil's dark eyes, to see his black soul… it's to fear him, and I deserve it.

Tonight's not one of my better nights, though. I got word that my rival on the East End, the head of the Libellula crime family, is trying to break out of being the main drug pusher in town and go into *my* business.

Part of the unspoken deal we've got between us is that the Sinners Syndicate deals in the three Gs: guns, girls, and gambling. Damien gets drugs and dough, including a pretty fit counterfeiting operation and a money-laundering op that does the Family well.

I don't mess with his business. Damien's not supposed to mess with mine. It's been that way for way too fucking long to change up now, but the whispers my guys have heard around the city tell me that, like Royce, he's pushing his luck.

Good thing I push *back*.

Which is why, when Royce flags down one of the newest waitresses, I know exactly what his bullshit is about tonight—and I'm ready for it.

Objectively, she's fucking stunning. All the girls at the Playground are. Wallets don't want to look at a jacked-up face when we're serving them fantasies unless she's got a massive set of tits or an ass that would have every joker nearly coming in his pants when she turns around. The tiny skirts and tight tops designed to draw a wandering eye toward their cleavage doesn't hurt, either.

A waitress can walk out of the Playground with a grand, easy, if she knows how to play the customers. One of the girls upstairs can triple that in half the amount of time if they're willing to take clients into the private rooms and do whatever the fuck the wallet wants. For a fifteen percent cut straight to the club, we provide the men, the space, and the protection, and the girls keep customers coming back for more.

This beauty is new meat. She doesn't have her

mark yet, and if she sticks around, I doubt she's the type who'll ever go from serving drinks to serving cunt, at least not for any regular customer. That's fine. We need all types here, even if I *don't*.

She's a redhead. Her curls are a deep, blood-red, the color so vivid it has to come from a salon, and they barely hit her shoulders. The style's on purpose, I'd bet. You can't miss the way the curls bounce or her tits jiggle as she curves her arm around her empty tray, nearly vibrating in place at the edge of our table.

Her eyes are brown.

Good.

For all his faults, Royce knows better than to shove a pair of green eyes in front of me, and whether the red is a dye job or not, I'd had a moment's pause as she stepped beneath the meager light that lets me see out while keeping most of my face in shadow.

She knows who she's facing. Even if Royce didn't already prime her—and I'd put a hundred bucks down he did—every one of my employees knows this booth belongs to me.

I'll give her some credit. Despite her obvious nerves and my shitty mood, her voice is a tremor-free purr as she asks, "Is there something I can get for you two gentlemen?"

Royce slides his gaze right toward me. "I'm good, but maybe Devil—"

"No." I flick my fingers at the waitress. It's pointless

to order another shot since I know damn well that's not what she's offering. "I'm not interested."

Her eyes dart to Royce. In the same light, his styled blond hair is almost golden, and as he offers her a smile, his teeth fucking *gleam*. "Thanks, Tessa. But that'll be all."

She nods quickly, curls and tits both bouncing wildly, before she flips her tray up and scampers away.

I should probably be offended at the stink of relief that clings to her. She must've thought for a moment that, after all the girls Royce has thrown at me, she'd be the one to tempt me enough to be chosen by the head Sinner.

Some of them actually wanted to fuck me. Others were probably willing to take one for the team, fucking me for either the money, the power, or because they could say they tamed Devil. And then there were those who thought they might be able to go through with it before realizing just who they were propositioning.

I already know which one she was. Tessa was so scared of my reputation, I'd wager she'd faint before I even got my cock out. And while somnophilia used to be an admitted kink of mine, I've only ever stuck my dick inside of a pussy I had permission to use whenever I wanted to.

Since I don't, she has nothing to worry about. Lucky for her and every other girl Royce tosses my way, the poor bastard is staying right where he is: trapped in my boxer briefs, waiting for my hand to give it a quick stroke whenever I can spare a few minutes away from business.

As gorgeous as she was, there's not a single twitch coming from down below. Maybe it's the headache, maybe it's the noise, and maybe it's knowing that she only approached the table because my second told her to, but I don't have the slightest urge to whack one out in my personal bathroom.

For some reason, that pisses me off even more.

"Royce." My voice comes out like a low growl. "You gotta stop with this shit."

Smart guy. He doesn't try to pretend not to know what I'm talking about.

"Can't help it. I'm worried about you, boss."

I snort. "Just because I'm not fucking a different girl every week like some of the men, doesn't mean there's something wrong with me. One of us has gotta run the syndicate with our brains, not our cocks."

"True, but getting laid every now and then won't hurt, either. Think of it as a way to blow off steam so you don't blow off one of our heads."

Dropping my hand to my lap, I run my thumb over the handle of my holstered Sig Sauer P365, my everyday carry. "I only kill those who deserve to die these days."

Royce is also smart enough not to have a comment about the 'these days' part of my statement, especially when he knows that I always have my firearm within reach.

I can't blame him for trying. He's got shit of his own he's trying to work out, and losing himself in a willing pussy for a night has helped him more times than I can count. He's not the only one in the syndicate who can't understand why I'm still single after all this time—why I don't take a mistress since I've made it clear I don't want a wife—even if he knows exactly *why* I'm the way I am.

It's for the same reason why he won't dangle a green-eyed, soft-spoken brunette on a hook in front of me to see if I'll take the bait. I won't, and it's not worth the fallout if I lose my temper.

Bad things happen when Devil's grip on his control slackens, and my second knows that better than anyone.

"Yeah," he says after a moment, light flashing off his expensive watch as he runs his fingers through his hair. "Sorry 'bout that, boss. I just thought—"

"Shut the fuck up."

Royce's teeth click as he snaps his mouth closed. He's a smart ass, yeah, but he's also an intuitive member of the syndicate. When he hears that snarl in my voice, he doesn't hesitate to obey.

I heard the buzz right before I felt the vibration coming from deep in the front pocket of my pants. The sensation is so unexpected that I completely tune out everything around me after I tell Royce to shut up. I can't do a damn thing about the *untz untz untz* of the music blaring around me, but here in the privacy of our booth, I can't focus with Royce yapping.

And, holy shit, I need to focus.

Because the buzz? It's not coming from the phone I placed face-down on the tabletop in front of me. It's in my pocket, and that means only one thing: the phone I've carried around for fifteen fucking years without it ringing once in the last thirteen or so is going off.

My heart stops for a beat before it starts to pound louder than the dance song playing.

Tanner set this phone up for me. I don't have any contacts in it, and every single number in the world except for two is blocked. I've kept it charged since I was a lovesick twenty-year-old, never changing the number even though I've had at least ten different business lines over the years. Anyone who wanted to reach me could find a way, but this number?

It's for one person only, and it's configured so that her personal cell and the landline she rarely uses could reach me if she wanted to.

And it's *ringing*.

I dip my fingers into my pocket, prepared for some spam caller to have found its way around Tanner's blocks. I know better than to get my hopes up. As much as I've never forgotten the one that got away, the last time Ava Monroe dialed my number, she told me she never wanted to see me again.

So she hasn't. Of course, that just means I got really good at watching her without her knowing I'm there, but though I held onto this phone—stubbornly transferring the line over the years just in case—I never honestly thought I'd see her number popping up on the screen.

I stare, not believing this is really happening.

Royce clears his throat. "Hey, Link?"

Just like how Royce is one of only two people who can push me without me pushing back, it's the same for calling me by my given name instead of the name given to me. He's earned that right, and he's the only one who ever dares to shorten my name from 'Lincoln' down to 'Link', except for—

Ava.

I squeeze my phone so tightly, I nearly crack the screen.

"Watch the club," I order. "I got to take this."

"Sure thing."

the life

Mrs. Crewes

FOUR
FIREFLIES

LINCOLN

Pocketing my business phone, I shove my body out of the booth, loose tie swaying as I start to push my way through the crowd.

It doesn't take more than two bodies stumbling away before the Playground recognizes that Devil's on the move. They clear a path for me, all while I'm muttering, "Shit, shit, shit," under my breath, hoping like hell that the phone keeps ringing.

I have two missed calls by the time I stalk past the guys at the door. Nodding at them, I step out into the night. There's still a line of wallets and fresh meat waiting to get in, but they all seem to have something else to look at when I turn my dark glare on them.

Four steps away from the club are all I can spare before I jab my thumb at the screen, dialing the number back. If she doesn't answer... if I missed talking to Ava for the first time in years because I couldn't fucking hear myself think over the pulsing music, I might put a bullet through the DJ just to get out my frustration.

Ava doesn't know it, but she saved his life tonight by answering on the second ring. How? Because the second I hear that it's her, she has all of my attention and that stills all my murderous thoughts for the moment.

Her voice is shaky and breathy as she gasps out, "Hello? Link? Is that you?"

Link...

A lump lodges in my throat. I swallow it roughly. "Yeah. It's me."

"Oh God, it's Ava. Ava Monroe. I... I don't know if you remember me—"

Remember her? The woman I've obsessed over for nearly half my damn life? Who haunts my dreams, stars in my nightmares, and is the closest thing I get to finding any pleasure in this fucked-up world when I stand outside of her place, watching her through the window, knowing that so long as she's safe, everything I've ever done—everything I've ever *lost*—is worth it?

"I remember you, Ava." It comes out short. I don't mean for it to, but I can't help myself as I demand in my gruff voice, "What is it you need?"

Because one thing for sure: if she's calling me now, she needs something. Whether it's from Lincoln

Crewes or the Devil of Springfield, I don't know—and I couldn't give a shit. Whatever she wants, it's hers.

And then she says, in a voice that's closer to a broken sob, "I need your help," and nothing else in the world matters.

You don't rise up through the ranks of an organized crime family before starting—and leading—your own syndicate without having a knack for taking control. Forcing myself to set aside the fact that this is Ava... *my* Ava... on the phone, I go right into 'boss' mode.

Keeping my questions to the point, I get as much information from Ava as possible before she dissolves into sobs that have my trigger finger itching. I promise her that I'll be right there, then wait until she hiccups "okay" before I kill the call and pocket the phone.

There are no contacts in that one. I've held onto it for the last fifteen years in case Ava ever needed me. Now that she has, I switch to my business phone.

In that one? When it comes to contacts, I have *hundreds*.

Most of the cops on my payroll are stored in my phone under nicknames; call me paranoid if you want, but you don't stay on top for long if you don't see enemies everywhere you look. If you go under the 'P' section, you'd find quite a few. The nicknames are self-explanatory, too. Unless they have a specific use to me, I keep them simple.

Pig 1.

Pig 2.

Pig - bald.

Pig - tiny dick energy...

Officer Burns, however, is different. If I ever thought I could sway him away from the benefits his badge and his uniform give him, I'd snap him up for the syndicate in a heartbeat. There's something dark in the steely-eyed cop I recognize, and if there's a single pig in all of Springfield I'd use for something like this, it's him.

I keep his number stored under 'W'. *Wildfire*. Nearly impossible to contain and easily set off with something as simple as a spark, it suits the cop, and not only because of his last name.

It's closing in on eleven. He usually patrols at night, though I haven't seen him around lately. Either way, if he sees my number popping up on his phone, he'll answer it if he wants his weekly deposits to keep on coming.

Three rings. It takes three rings, and then—

"This is Burns."

"It's me," I rumble.

"Devil. Haven't heard from you in a while. You okay?"

Better than I would've guessed a couple of minutes ago. "Just fine."

"Glad to hear it. What's up?"

"Remember how I got you that shot you were asking for a couple of months back?"

He should. Burns came to me because he needed a potent sedative loaded in an injector-driven syringe. Small enough to conceal in his palm, and strong enough to knock an average-sized woman on her ass.

I don't know why he wanted me to do it. Burns has his own way of seeing things, and while we both know that drugs are Damien's domain, he either couldn't get what he wanted from Libellula or he got his kicks seeing if I could get my hands on it.

Of course I could. There isn't a damn thing I can't get in Springfield, no questions asked for the right buyer, and I proved that when I handed over his sedative.

Burns is quiet for a moment before he says, "Yeah. I remember."

"Good. 'Cause now I need something from you."

"From Mace," he asks, "or from Officer Burns?"

"From the officer. And I need it tonight. You can do that?"

"Sarge has got me doing an overnight. I'm on duty 'til five, then I need to get my ass home. That good with you, Devil?"

"Yeah."

"You want flashy, or do you want quiet?"

I thinking about what Ava told me. "Bring the cruiser and the uniform. Lights are fine, but keep the sirens off. I don't want to wake up her neighborhood, not when my men are around."

"Got it." That's the best thing about Burns. I don't have to spell out that I need him in case of a cover-up and a personal crew of guys for the clean-up. He just knows. "Text me the address and I'm on my way."

In my experience, working with the SPD is pretty fucking easy. With enough money, all but the most righteous cop will look the other way when they have to. And maybe Burns has a cocky attitude that rubs me wrong, but even can I sense there's something off about him.

He reminds me of myself, and God only knows that's not a compliment.

"Will do. And I'll meet you there."

When we were still kids with an idyllic view of the future, Ava always said she wanted to get out of Springfield. We'd have a two-story house together, white picket fence, dog in the backyard... and we'd be the best of friends who shared a home because ten-year-old Ava couldn't comprehend the idea that she'd be my wife one day.

Ten-year-old Lincoln? I knew. I've known since the pretty little girl with pigtails and an impish grin joined my kindergarten class that she was mine.

At sixteen, she finally realized what I always

expected, giving me her heart, her virginity, and her promise that we would never break up.

At eighteen, she was still determined to get out of Springfield, and we started talking about marriage. About a family. About that same two-story house, with a room for just the two of us, where we could leave the city life behind.

At twenty, I fucked up. I fucked up so bad that I walked out of our apartment and never went back. Ava stayed for a few months, waiting for me to return, and when I *couldn't*, I thought I'd finally done enough to lose the only woman I'd ever love for good.

But while she eventually moved out of the apartment, she never left Springfield.

Like me, her roots are too deep.

Sometimes I think about what I would do if she finally did leave. Would I sacrifice everything I've built over the last fifteen years and follow her, even knowing that I destroyed all we had the night I was called *Devil* for the first time?

As I pull the nondescript black car I use whenever I want to stay under the radar up to the curb, I know the answer to that. I built my entire empire—from fighting for money, acting as a runner before I created the Sinners Syndicate, turning Jimmy's into the Devil's Playground—in the delusional hope that, one day, I might be good enough to beg Ava for a second chance.

There isn't a fucking thing I wouldn't do for this woman. She means more to me than my own life.

Ava might never have known it, but everything I do is with her in mind. Staying in the shadows, spying on her from the darkness, torturing myself by watching her date unworthy fuckers while I obsessed over her from just outside of her window... it's never mattered that I'm suffering if Ava is safe.

Over the years, she moved on as much as she could. While I was working over my competition, she went to college and got a respectable job as a first-grade teacher at Springfield Elementary. I traded my shitty apartment for the penthouse at Paradise Suites, and she scrimped and saved until she was able to buy a home for herself.

She still lives there today. Alone for now, since her last serious relationship ended about five years ago. She's had a couple of flings since—and it's taken every last bit of my resolve not to interfere—but, as far as I can tell, she's single these days.

Especially since she just killed one of her exes.

That's what I got out of her. In between gasps of air and half-sobs, Ava called me because she actually fired the gun I sent for her protection when she first moved into this house.

Part of her fear had to do with me. Sweet, innocent thing, she actually thought I'd send her a pistol that could be traced back to Lincoln Crewes. She shot it, but what if the gun was in my name? Would I get in trouble.

I couldn't care less about that regardless. Any

serials have been removed from all of the guns that pass through the syndicate, so I'm clear—but what had me speeding from the West Side of Springfield to the southern border is the realization that my Ava was in a position where she felt like she had to shoot to kill a man, ex or not.

I didn't ask her why she did it. At the time, it didn't matter. He was dead, Ava shot him, and he could've been the fucking Pope and I'd believe that she had a good reason to blow him away.

Now, as I fling open the driver's side door, climbing out of the car before easing it shut with my palm, I'm furious that Ava was in danger—and I wasn't there to protect her.

I know I can't always be. I got a business to run, the syndicate I'm responsible for, and it's not like Ava has any idea that I've kept tabs on her for longer than any sane man would.

But that's the thing. I'm *not* sane. When it comes to Ava Monroe, I never have been.

It's a quarter to midnight. The street is empty, a few lampposts dotting the residential area. Fireflies flicker in the patches of darkness.

My hands curl into fists at my side as a memory slaps me upside the head.

There was a small grassy field located in a lot between the apartment building we both lived in when we were kids and the skid row line-up with our favorite corner store, the 24-hour topless bar, liquor store, and laundromat. Ava's mom never wanted her to go past the lot, and with a little imagination, it was the closest thing we had to a park.

In the Julys of our childhood, that was the only spot in all of downtown Springfield where you'd see the faint green glow of the bugs winking on and off. There aren't any on the West Side, but seeing them on a muggy summer night like tonight...

I give my head a rough jerk and, stepping onto the curb, I turn right toward Ava's house.

the life

Mrs. Crewes

FIVE
IT'S ME

LINCOLN

It's the only one with a light on in the living room. Even if I didn't know which of the quaint, two-story houses was hers, it would have been easy to pick it out. It seems like the rest of the neighborhood is asleep.

Good.

She was terrified someone heard the gunshot, that one of her nosy neighbors would've called the cops, but she forgot that she still lives in Springfield. We don't rely on the cops here unless, like me, we can use them.

And if any report *did* come in, Burns will handle it. I'm not worried about that. Not worried about the missing cruiser, either. Of course I beat him here. My lead foot pressed down on the gas, I beat my fastest time across town by at least ten minutes.

There are two cars in the drive. The tiny white car is Ava's. I recognize the flashy red one, too. Her most recent lover was a smarmy mechanic named Joseph Maglione, also known as Joey. At thirty-four, a year younger than Ava and me, he lives in a place on the East End.

When I had Tanner run him, nothing popped. I still didn't like how he was an East Ender. That's Damien's territory, and I kept a closer eye on their relationship than the dentist she dated and the fellow teacher I actually thought she might marry.

It didn't last. After three months, they fizzled out, and the tightness in my chest whenever I knew Ava was involved with another man seemed to ease up a little.

Tonight? I might have yanked my tie off, tossing it in the back seat of my car despite leaving my suit jacket on in the muggy, summer heat, but I feel like I'm being fucking *squeezed.*

I missed something. That much is obvious as I cross her front yard in big steps, eager to reach her. Whatever happened tonight, I missed something and Ava was in danger.

Never fucking again, I promise as I lift my fist, rapping on the door.

She must have been waiting for me because, the

second the echo dies, I hear her sweet murmur come through the door.

"Who is it?"

Ava...

"It's me."

Over the pulse in my skull, I hear the scrape of the lock, the turn of the knob, a soft gasp as she pulls in the door, and then—

My heart breaks.

No. That's not right. The stone inside of my chest has been nothing but fault lines that splintered and spread from the moment I had to turn my back on this woman.

Having her look up at me with hope on her face and tears glistening in her eyes, it fucking *shatters*.

"Link. You came."

Of course I did.

"Are you going to let me in?"

Her gaze darts over my shoulder, looking at the quiet road. After a moment, she sighs, then nods. "Uh, yeah. Of course. Please."

Ava backs away, leaving me enough room to maneuver my bulk through her doorway.

It reeks in here. Of blood and death and shit, with a hint of fear and the acrid stink of vomit. It wouldn't take someone in my line of business to know something bad went down, even without the corpse in the middle of her living room.

Jesus Christ. All I got out of Ava was that she used

the gun I bought her to shoot an intruder in her house, and that while she swore it was self-defense—not that I would've cared either way—I'm beginning to think it was a little more than that.

Vividly aware of her quickened breaths behind me, I force myself to look away from her for the moment. She called me for help. She didn't call me because she finally, *finally* realized that she's the one that got away, or that I've spent fifteen years waiting for the goddamn phone I've carried around with me to ring. So she called me Link on the phone before. It's not Link she needs—it's Devil, and I know how to be him far better than the type of man who can take this beautiful, distraught creature and calm her down.

Tugging my suit jacket around me, I allow my gaze to flicker over the room. I've only seen it from outside the window—though I've been working with Tanner to find a way to get cameras in here like I had in her last apartment—but it has Ava's stamp on every bit of it. From the cozy furniture to the oak coffee table in the middle of the room, the TV mounted on the wall, and the lush carpet covered in blood and brains, it's hers, and I'm viscerally angry that the blood and brains and dead bastard cooling on the floor have ruined it for her.

He's on his back, half his face blown away. There's a towel next to him, spread out on the carpet, but he's the ugliest fucking fixture in the middle of her room.

Now, I've seen my share of DBs. Been responsible

for most of them, too. A little blood and guts do nothing to affect me, but when Ava moves just enough that she's not only in my line of sight, but standing beneath the light, my whole body goes tight.

Her hair is mussed. She never leaves this house with a single strand out of place, and even when she's spending the day in, she prides herself on her hair. Her t-shirt is hanging off one shoulder. Her tiny shorts are twisted.

I look at her face. Deceptively innocent, but still the most gorgeous woman I've ever seen before— whether at twenty when I was last with her, or now at thirty-five—I know every inch of her intimately. From the freckle over her lip to the way her right eyelashes are a shade darker than her left, I *know* Ava.

And my Ava doesn't have red marks dotting her cheeks like that. Four of them, one on her left cheek, three on the other, someone squeezed her face hard enough to leave an imprint behind. By morning, they'll be bruises, but the red stands out to me now.

An intruder, huh? I knew there was something more to it when I recognized her ex's car outside, but what exactly did that fucker break into her house to do tonight? Pretty single woman who attracts the worst sort of darkness in a man... whose clothing is disheveled, and who had to pull a trigger to get him to stop?

Almost as a reflex, I slip my hand beneath my suit

jacket, patting the Sig in my holster, making sure I still have it at the ready.

She killed him, but if she hadn't? I would have.

And I would have drawn it out a lot longer than a single merciful bullet to the face.

Something must have passed over mine because Ava draws a few steps away from me, even more frightened than before.

I don't want her to regret calling me. Pulling the expressionless mask I'm known for onto my features, I move past her, getting a better look at the man she killed.

My gaze is drawn to the tattoo winking up at me.

Fuck!

How did I miss it before?

Shit, I *know* how. Already having Ava nearby has me making stupid mistakes because there's no other explanation for me missing the dark ink on the bastard's forearm during my earlier sweep. It's not like it's hidden. When his dead body crumpled on the floor, his arm splayed out, and there it is.

A dragonfly.

Damien Libelulla's symbol that he has inked on every member of his Family.

I swallow my curse and barely restrain the urge to bloody my shoe, kicking the worthless piece of shit's corpse away from me. Only knowing I'd make a bigger mess in Ava's living room—and probably scare her further—keeps me from giving in to my rage.

I thought she was off-limits. For fifteen years, I made it clear that none of my men would ever target Ava. Most of the soldiers thought it was because she was a respected teacher at Springfield Elementary, while those higher up in the syndicate guess there's more to it than that. Only my underboss has any clue that I've spent the last fifteen years watching her from the shadows—and that's because Royce caught me doing it a couple of summers ago.

But I made a mistake. A big one.

She was off-limits to my syndicate, yeah.

What about Damien's Family?

Walking back over to the front door—no Burns yet, but he'll be here soon—I close the door behind me and turn the lock. Then, nodding at Ava, I sidle past her again. I keep my face turned away so that she can't see the murder in my gaze; as fragile as she is right now, I can't risk her thinking the look is meant for her.

Snagging the tousled blanket hanging off the back of her couch, I snap my wrist, covering the corpse with it.

I'll buy her a new blanket. I'll buy her a hundred. But, right now, I'm not going to make Ava stay in this room with the remains of that bastard out in the open, a reminder to both of us that she was forced to protect herself.

"I... thank you. I— I didn't think to cover Joey."

So, I was right. The car out front... knowing it was one of Ava's exes... everything added up to the dead bastard being her last boyfriend—but I have to double-check.

"Joey Maglione?"

Ava frowns. "Uh... yeah, actually." Understanding is slow to dawn, and when it does, she trembles. "Shit, Link, did you know him? Was he your friend? Oh my God—"

"He wasn't my friend," I tell her, using enough force to bring her back from the brink.

That's true. Even if I already would've considered anyone with a dragonfly tat an enemy just because they're part of the Libellula Family and I'm a Sinner, I hated Joey Maglione for a whole other reason.

He had Ava. One of the lucky few she chose after I gave her up, if only for a few months at the beginning of this year, he could call Ava *his*... and I couldn't.

I knew all about them. I knew whenever she got a new boyfriend, partner, lover, fling. I'd had Tanner run this one, too, and he came back clean enough. No tracable ties to any crime rings in Springfield, but whether our intel was old or he recently joined up, it doesn't matter. Someone fucked up and now Ava is paying the price.

A Dragonfly in her cozy home. It could be because they found out she had ties to me, or it could just be coincidence. Either way, he hurt her, now he's dead, and she needs me.

I gesture for her to take a seat on the couch. Shaky, distraught, her pretty green eyes haunted and glazed, she trips over her feet, dropping down on the farthest cushion. Following her lead, giving her some space, I brace my twitchy fingers against the couch's arm.

"Okay, Ava. I'm here now." I'll take care of *everything*. "Just, first, tell me what the fuck that prick did to you."

the life

Mrs. Crewes

SIX
PROPOSAL

AVA

I don't realize just how much I expected Link to blame me for what happened until I finish telling him all about it and the only thing he says when I'm done is, "Good. Fucker deserved it."

I blink, stunned. Having him here, sitting on my couch in his fancy get-up, oozing confidence and an "I've fucking got this" attitude, I've calmed down a little. The way he covered Joey's body helps, too, and I only stumbled a few times when I got to the point in my story where he grabbed my face, tripping me to the floor, then shoving his hand up my shorts.

Link did stop me there. His eyes—impossibly black compared to the deep brown I remember—seemed to burn as he leaned forward in his seat, asking, "Did he..."

He doesn't use the word. *Rape*. He doesn't have to, either. It's obvious what Joey's intentions were, and while I shot him before he could, I was still assaulted and we both know it.

But he never got his dick out so I shook my head, and Link didn't push. He just waited for me to finish.

So I did. I called him because I needed his help, and he can't do anything until he knows exactly what he's dealing with. The way he reacted so blasé when he found Joey on the floor just proves that he was the only one I *could* call.

Who else would shrug over a dead body like it was nothing the way he did?

This is part of his job, right? This is what he does. People die—and I'm not so naive to think he's not responsible for some—and he makes them disappear.

Link can make Joey disappear, too.

He already told me to stop peering over my shoulder, peeking through the blinds, watching to see if the cops are going to roll up to my house. I'd been expecting them from the moment the shot echoed through my house. I ended up turning the television back off after I hung up with Link. Either they were coming or not, and the blaring volume on the set was adding to my jumpiness.

They are coming. At least, *one* is, but Link said it's okay. If he gives the word, the cop will help him, and I know I shouldn't believe anything a gangster says, but this is *Link*.

Even if he's all grown up now.

I'm still in shock. I have to be. I freaking killed a man tonight, and while that keeps on running on repeat in the forefront of my mind like a song I can't get out of my head, I can't help but marvel at what a man Lincoln Crewes has become.

Is it the shadow of a beard on his strong jaw? His chiseled features, so wild and untamed and fierce despite the suit trying to contain him? It can't. Looking at him, facing him from opposite sides of the couch, I notice that the first three buttons on his white shirt are undone, giving me a peek at his tanned chest and part of the tattoo he has hidden beneath it.

His suit jacket has fallen open. I don't know if he wants me to see the gun perched dangerously at his hip, but though I started when I did, it's... it's *different* than the open threat Joey made, keeping his gun on his thigh. Link has it because he's a dangerous man, and while I know he'd pull it in a heartbeat if he felt he had to, it's as much an accessory on him as his tattoo.

Link's hair is shorter than it used to be. That adds to his dangerous air, losing any of the softness he once had. His body is bigger, muscles more prominent as they bulge beneath the suit. He still has a brawler's hands, I think to myself, looking at his thick knuckles.

You can take the fighter out of downtown Springfield, dress him up, give him power and money... and, deep down, I want to believe he's still the same kid who would fight in the back alley for twenty bucks and a pizza to bring home to our apartment.

I want to believe that—but then I dare to look directly into his dark eyes, seeing nothing but the promise of retribution and barely stifled fury without any of the love my Link once felt for me, and I know this isn't Link at all.

This is the Devil of Springfield, and I'm at his mercy.

I gulp. He frowns.

"Hey," he asks, pushing his big body off of my couch. "You still drink that tea shit?"

Back during my college days, when anxiety over exams got to be too much, I settled my nerves with a steaming mug of chamomile tea. Link never touched the stuff, but he was always my biggest supporter. At the first sight of one of my freak-outs, he would start brewing a cup.

I nod.

"Where do you keep it? In the kitchen?"

"Yes," I tell him.

Without another word, he starts across the living room, walking past Joey without a single look, though he does pause when he reaches my spread-out dish towel.

He goes to toe the towel with his dress shoe.

"No. Don't do that." At his look, I feel a wave of shame rush through me. "Puke's under there," I explain. "I threw up my dinner."

And the most I could do while I waited for Link was cover it up with a towel. I left Joey's destroyed face on display, but tossed a dish towel over my vomit because I couldn't bring myself to clean it up while I waited to see if Link would show.

"Understandable," he says, stepping over the towel. "I'll get someone to clean that up when they come for the body."

Does that mean he's really going to help me? When all he said was that Joey deserved his fate, he didn't add anything about what I should do now, and I wasn't sure how to ask.

I don't get the chance now, either. He pushes the doors to my kitchen in like he owns the house, vanishing into the other room.

Part of me thinks I should get up and follow him. The other part feels weighed down by fear and stress and something I can't quite understand right now, so I stay seated on my couch, not sure what else to do while I hear my former love move around my kitchen.

He's gone for about six or seven minutes, and I spent that entire time realizing something. At first, it hits me that I didn't tell him that I keep my tea bags in the cabinet over my fridge, or that my mugs are on the other side of the kitchen. I have a teapot that I keep stored in a lower cabinet, but he didn't ask about that, either.

And that's not all.

I never told him where I lived, or where to find me.

But after I called him, he was here in no time at all. Maybe I could explain that away as him looking me up on the internet or something before he hopped in his car, but what about the gun...

I told Link I used it. He'd asked how I got my hands on a "piece", wondering if I killed Joey with his own gun, but after I pointed out that the much larger gun was still where my ex hadn't been able to reach it, I admitted that I fired the pocket pistol Link sent me all those years ago.

He didn't deny it. When I called it his gift, he sat there with an unreadable expression on his handsome face, waiting for me to continue.

Because Link already knew where I lived. He'd sent me a weapon through the mail right after I moved in, and now he's in my kitchen, going through my things as though he belongs in there.

As though he never left me.

When Link returns, he's carrying my favorite mug in one of his big hands. Reaching the couch where I'm still sitting, he holds it out to me.

I take it.

"Drink."

"I like to let it steep a little longer," I murmur.

"I know." Glancing up at him through the fringe of my lashes, he says, "I remember. But then you're going to drink, pet."

Pet.

My eyes drop back to the steam wafting over my tea.

Pet...

Link might have called me 'Saint Ava' when we were kids, but when we started dating more seriously in high school, he developed this habit of calling me all sorts of pet names, seeing which one would stick. My name only has three letters—and my middle name, Marie, is no better—so it's not like I had any real options for nicknames. Lincoln had 'Link', and he wanted a name of his own for me.

I was 'sweetheart' and 'baby', 'honey' and 'my Ava', but the one he teased me with more than the others was 'pet' because he would put on this ridiculous British accent whenever he did.

He didn't just now. Instead, with a deep rumble to his voice, and an expectation that he'll be obeyed, the term of endearment rolls off of his tongue so easily, it makes me wonder how many other 'pets' he's had since he left me—or currently has.

I try to shove that thought out of my head. It's bad enough that my gaze instinctively landed on the ring finger on his left hand earlier, searching for a wedding ring. I was being ridiculous if—for even a moment—I got jealous over the women in Link's life when I haven't been a part of it for so long. That was his decision, after all, and he wanted me to move on.

Sometimes I wonder if I ever did...

Red and blue lights suddenly flash into the living room from between the slats in my window blinds.

My hand sloshes as I jump, sending scalding tea onto my thigh. It burns my skin, causing me to yelp as I try to steady both my mug *and* my racing heart.

Eyes dipping to my thigh, Link frowns again. "Are you okay?"

I'm not worried about the burn from the tea. "There's a cop out there."

"I know. You stay here. I'll take care of it."

I'm so freaking glad to hear that. Setting my mug down on the arm of my couch, clasping my fingers together, I offer him a small smile and finally tell him what I'd been meaning to since he rushed over: "Thank you, Link."

To my surprise, his jaw goes tight. "Don't thank me. You haven't asked me what I want for payment yet."

What? Payment?

Of course. Link didn't get to the top of the food chain in Springfield by doing jobs for free, whatever they are. He came because an old girlfriend called him, half-hysterical. That didn't mean that he was doing it out of the kindness of his heart. He wants payment.

I can only imagine how much this is going to cost me.

"I have four thousand in the bank. If I cash out my retirement, that's another ten, I guess. I know that's not much, but—"

"I don't want your money," he says, cutting me off.

Oh. "Then what do you want?"

I don't have much, but my car is pretty decent. My house, too. I have a little jewelry, if that's what he means, or—

"*You*."

The corner of his mouth twitches enough to be noticeable. It's the first sign of amusement I've seen from him since he walked through my door and I tell myself he has to be kidding.

"Me?" I give a tiny laugh of my own. "What do you mean, *me*?"

"It's very simple. I need a wife—"

"And you don't have one already?"

I'm not sure if I sound relieved to hear that, or irrationally pleased. I shouldn't have any reaction at all, but so surprised by the direction this conversation has taken, I give myself away.

Link shakes his head. "That's the problem. As the head of the syndicate, I'm expected to have one. To turn the Sinners into a family, right? Can't do that without a wife, and I've been too busy to find one. And here you are. No husband. No boyfriend," he adds, and I can't help but wonder how he knows *that*, "and no way out of this unless you say 'yes'."

"Link… you can't be serious."

"Dead fucking serious," he agrees.

"Marry you… that's your price. You want me to *marry* you?"

He nods.

Lifting my mug to my lips, I swallow a mouthful of tea. It's still hot and I'm probably scalding the roof of my mouth and the length of my esophagus, but I force it down. Right now, I need the calm it provides.

"Careful, pet," he says softly. "Easy."

Easy? *Easy*? I've got a dead man—that I *killed*—in my living room, a cop pulled up at my curb, and my former lover-turned-gangster freaking *proposing* to me... and he wants me to take it easy?

That's not what he's doing. Not really. The proposing part, I mean. Link didn't suddenly realize after all these years that he made a mistake and he still loves me.

Oh, no.

I'm just a single woman who is desperate enough to even entertain this insanity.

And I *am*.

"So... if I say 'yes', it would be a fake marriage. Like a marriage of convenience, one of those in name only. Just so people stop wondering when you'll find a wife... right?"

Link shakes his head. "It'll be real from the moment you say 'I do', pet."

Okay. He must've taken one too many punches to the face when he was younger because I'm beginning to think Link's the crazy one now.

And yet, I can't stop myself from asking, "What would I have to do?"

"I'll need an heir one day." There's no small smile

twitching his lips any longer. Link is really freaking serious. "Someone to take over the syndicate for me, with hellfire in their veins and the devil in their blood. With you as their mother, at least they'll have some good in them, too."

My heart is thumping, and I'm back to being too stunned to decipher why. "Children," I sputter. "You want children?"

"Eventually. Why? Is that a problem?"

I don't even know how to answer *that*. Acting the part of his wife in front of his gang is one thing, but sleeping with him? Having children with him?

Spending the rest of my life with the man who broke my heart when I was a silly little girl who still believed in fairy tale endings? A man who is blackmailing me into marriage in exchange for helping me get through the second worst night in my life?

As if he knows exactly what I'm thinking, he crouches down so that we're on the same level.

"You'll be my wife in all ways, and this whole night... all of it... it can just go away."

If only it was that simple.

"Link, I—"

A shadow passes across his face. "They call me Devil."

'They' might. To me, he's always been Link.

"I know that, but—"

"Just making sure you do. Because if you say 'yes', I want you to know who you'll be tied to." He waits a moment, then adds, "Who will be able to protect you as your husband should."

Oh, he's good. Link always was even when he *was* good. But Devil... he knows exactly what card to play, and that I have a shit hand of my own.

He wants a wife. I need protection.

From retaliation from the Libellula Family. From the law. From my own conscience... I need *him*.

It's a devil's bargain, and I can't see any way but to agree.

"If I say 'yes', I'll be safe?" I ask. "No one will come after me for what I did?"

Not Damien? Not the police?

Not anyone?

Nodding once, Link holds out his hand, palm side up.

Knowing what he wants, I lay my hand on his.

He folds his calloused fingers around mine, then rises up to his full height. Once standing, he gives my hand a tug, helping me to my feet.

We're so close, we're basically breathing the same air for a moment before he tugs again, pulling me up against his hard chest.

With his hand a possessive brand on my back, Link's chin pinning me against him as he rests it on my head, he rubs the edge of his thumb along the height of my cheek.

"I promise you this, pet: no one will touch you when Devil marks you as his."

the life

Mrs. Crewes

SEVEN
OUR WEDDING

LINCOLN

With Ava in my arms again, it takes everything in me to let her go.

I have to, though. Officer Burns turned off the flickering lights on the top of his cruiser, but he's out there. Someone has to go talk to him, and since I'm using my connections as leverage to force her into agreeing to marry me, I need to get out there.

I give myself a few more seconds. Stroking her hair, I have to stifle my shudder at just how fucking soft it is. If my cock hadn't already gone hard just from touching her hand, her hair would've been enough to get me ready to fuck through a steel beam.

That's why I purposely angle my hips away from her. Until we make it so that it's 'til death do we part, I can't scare her. I also can't give her any reason to change her mind. If she knows how badly I want to fuck her, especially after that Dragonfly bastard thought he could, she might actually take her chances with the crooked Springfield cops.

I'd never let her. She doesn't know that, but even if she refused my offer, I'd help her.

Then I'd marry her anyway, and she'd just have to get used to it. At least, this way, she thinks she has a say in whether she agreed or not, and fuck if I'm not going to use that, too.

Fake marriage... Ava really thought she could get away with a *fake* marriage to me. No fucking way. I've always been an "all or nothing" kind of man, and now that I have my second chance ripe for the taking, I'm going to snatch it—and nothing is going to stop me.

But, first, I have to marry her. And in order to do that, I've got to do my job.

Already there are so many things I have to take care of, and the first one is going out to make sure Officer Burns can handle the cop side of what went down tonight. As for clean-up, I got guys for that.

Then I guess I'm going to go get hitched.

And, for the first time since I joined the life, I'll do it by the book. I need my marriage to Ava to be legal. When so much of my life is spent on the other side of the line, when it comes to her, I won't drag her into my darkness any more than I already have.

Thinking about the business phone in my pocket as I continue to hold her close, I smile to myself.

Good thing I have a judge or three who owes me a favor.

Ava is sleeping when I finally let myself back into her house.

I'm not surprised. It's well after midnight now, and her adrenaline from earlier must have finally worn off. The chamomile tea wouldn't have helped, either, especially since I brewed two tea bags for her instead of one.

I used to do that all the time. One would help with her nerves, two would help her sleep, and I hadn't been planning on forcing Ava to marry me when I was getting her tea shit ready for her. Oh, no. That spark of fucking brilliance came when I thought of walking out of her house, passing the problem onto a couple of my men, and returning to my empty bed, familiar hand, and a life where Ava Monroe was a ghost and not a living, breathing, gorgeous woman in front of me.

I told her. I told her what she was getting into. Who she would be marrying if she agreed to be mine. They don't call me Devil for nothing, and if I have to coerce her into being my bride, I will.

Anything to have her. To hold her. To keep her close.

To protect her.

To fuck her.

To *love* her.

She's mine. She always was, and she's always been, and now that I finally have the excuse to tie her to me for life, damn right I'm going to do it.

As Devil's wife, she'll be *untouchable*. Even if Damien and his crew decide to go after her for what went down, he'll have to go through me and the entire syndicate for a chance—and that will never fucking happen.

After I told Burns what I needed him to do, I called up Royce. As my second, he's the closest thing in this world to someone I trust, and now that Ava's involved, that's essential. I gave him his instructions, too, and proving once again that there's no better 'fixer' in the game right now, Royce got me what I needed even before the rest of the clean-up crew he assigned started out from the West Side.

I was very clear. While Burns was keeping an eye on the legal side of things with the other cops, the clean-up crew wasn't going to set foot inside of Ava's house until we were already gone. They would take care of the body and the mess, though I don't think she realizes that she won't be coming back here.

Once she's mine, I'll lock her in my penthouse if that's what it takes to keep her safe. Good thing that school's out for the summer because there's no way in fucking hell she'll be going anywhere that I don't have eyes on her twenty-four/seven.

She'll get over it. She'll have to. Ava will figure out

that I'm doing this all for her—for me, too, yeah, but mainly for her—whether she agrees with it or not.

I'm in charge of the syndicate. I'll be in charge of this marriage, too, and the sooner she realizes that, the better.

Taking the dry cleaner's bag from Royce, I tell him to park around the corner and wait in his car until I'm gone. The others are going to station themselves a couple of streets over, heading toward Ava's house on foot, but Royce had pulled up right behind Burns's cruiser so that he didn't have to lug the bag through backyards and side streets with him.

Inside, I lay the bag down on the far end of the couch once I see that Ava is curled up on her side, snuffling softly, pillowing her cheek on her hands. She looks so innocent, and I almost think twice about what I'm doing.

Almost.

Leaning down at her side, I trace the edge of her cheek. "Time to get up, pet."

Her eyelids flutter, a soft moan falling from her lips, as she continues to sleep.

I should let her. If I call him back and tell him to, Judge Callihan will clear his schedule and marry us in the morning. There's no reason why I have to do this *now*. Ava gave her word. The girl I used to know would rather cut out her tongue than break a promise. She said she'd marry me, and I should let her get through the trauma of tonight before pushing her into this.

I should—but I'm not going to.

A little firmer, I pat her cheek. "Ava? Ava."

She finally opens her eyes, staring up at me with that same dazed look in her eyes. For a moment, I get the feeling that she doesn't recognize me, before she says in a voice rough with sleep, "Link? You're back?"

Yes, pet. And now that I have you with me, you'll never be away from me again...

"It's time to go."

She starts to sit up, even as she asks, "Where are we going?"

"Out of the house. I've got a crew coming and we shouldn't be here for it."

"Joey," she breathes out. She closes her eyes. "It wasn't a nightmare, was it?"

The sooner she understands that, the better. "No."

"But what about—"

"Don't worry about any of it," I tell her, taking her hand again. I'm already addicted to the feel of her hand in mine, skin to skin, and I can't fucking wait until I get this woman naked. "While we're gone, my cop's got this covered."

"Your cop?"

"He's on my payroll," I explain. That should be enough. "He's going to stay parked out front. Anyone who heard anything and is still up might be curious if they see the cruiser, but he knows how to handle them if they start asking questions. My guys will take care of the trash in your house. As for us," I add, using her hand to pull her to a standing position again, "we have an appointment."

"An appointment," Ava echoes. "Isn't it like two in the morning?"

It's a quarter to one, but that doesn't matter. "Exactly, which is why we shouldn't keep the judge waiting."

He will. The entire Springfield court is either in my pocket or Damien's, and Judge Callihan is one of mine. For the amount that I've already lined his with, he'll stay up all night if I tell him to, and he'll do it with a smile on his grumpy, old face.

Of course, *Ava* doesn't know that—and I'm not about to enlighten my pretty little bride to that fact.

"Judge... I'm sorry. I'm so tired that none of this is making sense to me."

I know, pet. I know, and while that wasn't my intention, I'm not going to apologize for it, or not use it to my advantage.

"You can nap in the car. But first..." I grab the dry cleaner bag containing the white dress in Ava's size that Royce managed to come up with and offer it out to her. "Go get ready. Pack a bag with whatever you think you'll need for a couple of days, then put this on. We'll leave when you're ready."

"Ready?" she asks. "Ready for what?"

I give her a predatory grin, one I absolutely mean.

"For our wedding."

the life

Mrs. Crewes

EIGHT
I DO

AVA

The judge's robes are askew.

The entire time he's going through the shortened version of a civil marriage ceremony, that's all I can focus on. His robes are askew, and he's yawning.

It's two o'clock in the morning. I'm standing in the small office in Judge Callihan's mansion in North Springfield. A mousy-looking man in his early fifties, he has the dazed look of a man ripped out of his sleep so that he can marry me to Lincoln Crewes.

Oh, wait. That's because he *is*.

Link wastes no time. Proving that he has infinite connections, once I had traded my pajamas for the lacy, white wedding dress—that, somehow, is just my size—and a pair of white flats I found in the back of my closet, I ran a brush through my hair while he made a few phone calls. Twenty minutes after he woke me up from my own sleep, I was in a car driven by a man whose face I never saw, sitting next to Link, fiddling with the floofy skirt on the dress he gave me.

Up until he led me up the walkway to Judge Callihan's house, I didn't honestly believe I would be getting married tonight. It was one thing for him to dangle his help and his protection in front of me in exchange for saying I would marry him; it's another thing entirely for him to expect me to pledge myself to him immediately.

But that's exactly what he expected. Link even had a simple gold band for the occasion that he slipped on my finger after I—almost in a daze—say 'I do'. Link's version is a lot more adamant, so much so that the judge glanced up at him in surprise when he growled it out.

The judge had a printout waiting for us, too. He laid it out on his desk, and once we exchanged vows, all that was left to make our quickie marriage binding was the officiant witnessing us signing the license.

Is it legal? Probably not. I always thought you needed a separate witness, but both Link and his judge seemed satisfied, and it's not like I can really question them. Even if I did, what good would it do?

My new husband is the head of an organized crime syndicate. I guess I should be grateful he was pretending to do things by the book at all.

Link took the pen first, writing his legal name on one line. Passing the pen to me, he watched closely as I signed it with a trembling hand, swooping *Ava Monroe* on the line.

The judge takes the sheet. "Congratulations, Mr. and Mrs. Crewes."

When I was a senior in high school, I used to doodle *Ava Crewes* and *Mrs. Crewes* in the margins of my spiral notebook. Little hearts surrounded the name I always thought I might have one day, but gave up on many years ago. It's so strange to think of that now, and I barely have a second for that to sink in before Link snatches my fingers.

With a nod, he says, "I appreciate it. Next time you're at the Playground, let me know. I'll take care of you."

Judge Callihan's tired eyes light up at Link's solemn promise. "If there's anything else I can do for you..."

"There is. You can tell me where your nearest bathroom is."

"Of course. Down the hall, third door on the left."

"Thanks. And don't worry about showing us out, Judge. When we're done, we'll let ourselves out."

The judge gives him a knowing smile. "I'll send one of my staff to lock up in... half an hour or so? Or would an hour be better?"

Link tucks my hand beneath his arm, tugging me into his side. "Half an hour should be fine. I just want to finalize our marriage as soon as possible."

"Yes, yes. I understand." He finally adjusts his crooked robes. "I'm sure I'll see you soon."

"Come, Ava," Links says, completely disregarding the judge. "This way."

I guess he doesn't want to leave me behind with Judge Callihan while he takes a trip to the bathroom. Considering he thinks he'll need it for close to half an hour, I figure Link wants to take a shit before we leave, and I'm prepared for him to park me in the hall before he slips inside of the bathroom alone.

Only that's not what happens.

As soon as we reach the bathroom, Link pushes the door in with his free hand, using his grip on mine to pull me in behind him. Once he has, he finally lets go of me, but he closes the door before I can step back out into the hall again.

With a decisive turn of the lock, he traps me in the small room with him.

It's a single toilet bathroom, with a large mirror, two cabinets, and an oversized porcelain sink. Smelling of potpourri, with every single decoration lacking personality and screaming "money", it's a nice bathroom—but it's obviously designed for one person to use it at a time.

"I'll wait in the hall," I begin.

"Not so fast, pet," he says, his voice a low rasp. "Come here."

I gulp. "Link, you probably want privacy for this."

"Yeah, and that's why I brought you to the bathroom instead of just bending you over Callihan's desk."

What? "I don't understand."

"A lapsed Catholic is still a Catholic," he says, shoving his suit jacket and his sleeve up just enough for me to see a hint of the rosary he has tattooed on his forearm, toward his wrist. "I didn't get to marry my wife in a church, but fuck if I'm not going to consummate this marriage right now. Then you'll really be mine."

Consummate...

Holy shit. "Link, you don't mean—"

"That I'm going to fuck you right now? That's exactly what I mean. Unless you'd rather take back your vows and I take back my offer of protection."

Asshole. He knows there's no going back for me. Either Damien Libellula and his goons come after me for killing one of their own, or I go to jail for murder. Maybe I get manslaughter, or even a lesser charge since I did it in self-defense, but what about the unregistered gun in my house? I'm absolutely fucked if I walk away from Link now.

Then again, I'm absolutely fucked if I stay in this bathroom—and this marriage—with him.

What's that saying? Better the devil you know?

What does that mean when the man looming over you *is* the Devil?

"Lincoln—"

"Understand me, Ava: once I fuck you, you *are* my wife. This is your last chance to change your mind. I said 'til death do you part in Callihan's office—and I mean it. You have to mean it, too, or else I walk away right now and you're on your own." He tilts his head toward me, too gorgeous for his own good. "So what will it be? Yes or no?"

God damn it, he knows that I'm already in too deep to even think about refusing him. Worse, the idea of being with him again... I don't hate it.

I don't hate it at all.

I gulp, swallowing back my nerves—and my growing lust. "Yes."

"Then turn around."

I do.

"Good girl," he murmurs. "Now brace your hands on the sink and hold on tight."

Ignoring the lump lodging in my throat again, I do that, too.

I don't know why I'm so surprised, but it hurts a little that Link can't even look me in the eye when we have sex for the first time as a married couple. If I had any delusions that he picked me to be his wife because he had any lingering feelings for me, they die a quick death as he bends down behind me.

Throwing the skirts of my white dress up, he grabs my panties and starts to tug them down. He keeps going until he's crouched down behind me, the panties around my ankles.

"Lift," he barks.

I lift.

Once my panties are off, the echo of Link's zipper being tugged downward fills the small bathroom. I swallow nervously at the whisper of his slacks moving, knowing that he's only undressing us enough to release his cock and line it up with me.

He lifts the skirts again, placing them against my back so that my bare ass is on display. Leaning over me, trapping the skirts between our bodies, I stare into the basin of the sink as I wait for this to be over with.

This isn't making love. What's going to happen next is fucking, plain and simple, and I don't feel like his bride. I don't even feel like his former lover. Right now, I'm just a pussy to him, something he'll use to get off, and to make it so that I know just what I signed away when I scrawled my name on the marriage license.

And that's when Link orders, "Eyes up, pet. I want you to watch as I make you mine for life."

My eyes shoot to the mirror. I've never seen such a self-satisfied grin on Link's face until now. For a second, I almost regret thinking so poorly about him—this isn't the first time he got off, the two of us watching as he fucked me—but then I see the muscles beneath his suit jacket move, sense something blunt and hard nudging at the entrance of my pussy, and all I can think about is how this is really happening.

How he's going to just take off my underwear, pull down his zipper, throw up the skirts of my borrowed dress, and shove himself inside of me without any foreplay, any sweet caresses, or any protection.

I won't deny that I've always been turned on by a powerful guy who took charge. It's also no secret that I'm never hotter than when I'm fooling around in a place I shouldn't be. Whether it was making out beneath the bleachers at school, or how the first time me and Link ever had sex was in Marissa Reilly's bathroom during her Sweet Sixteen, I might be a little shocky over tonight, but my pussy's already soaked.

But protection...

"Wait—"

"I've done my waiting," Link murmurs under his breath, but he keeps his cock lodged just past my entrance without pushing any further in.

I have no idea what that means. It's barely been an hour since he blackmailed me into marrying him, and if he can't go an *hour* between getting off, I'm in trouble. Maybe when I was twenty, I could keep up with a libido like that, but I haven't had sex in almost a year.

I've been tested since then, but I'm not on any birth control. Even when I was dating, I insisted on any of my partners wrapping it up. I haven't let a guy go bareback in me since... well, *Link*.

I don't want to think about how many women he's been with over the years. When we were each other's one and only, I had no problem letting him do whatever he wanted to do to me. Now? I can't hold the years against him—especially when I'm in this situation because of an ex of my own—but that doesn't mean I'm going to let him fuck me bare.

I'm not getting out of being railed in this bathroom. That much is obvious. He wants our quickie marriage consummated, and I'm so in over my head that I have no choice but to go along with it.

But damn if I'm not going to ask about protection first.

"Condom," I gasp out, my entrance stretching slightly as he shifts his stance behind me, cock slipping a half-inch in. "Please tell me you have a condom."

Reaching in front of me, Link collars my throat. He bends his head, pressing a hot, open-mouth kiss to the side of my neck. "Why the fuck would I have a condom?"

I insisted my lovers wear one for protection—I guess his didn't.

The skirt of the wedding dress is a slight buffer between us as Link leans over me. In this position, he has me completely trapped. One jerk of his hips and he'll be fully seated, leaving me no escape.

I don't want to. Everything happened so quickly tonight, but I'd be lying if I said that it doesn't feel... feel *right* to be in Lincoln Crewes's arms again, to feel the weight of his bulk behind me, his heat searing my skin.

But just because I'm irrationally looking forward to fucking him again, that doesn't mean that I don't want to be safe.

Before I can articulate that, he nibbles on my ear lobe, sucking my silver hoop into his mouth. A husky chuckle bathes my neck with intoxicating warmth as he releases it before he murmurs wickedly, "Told you, pet: if I knock you up, I need an heir anyway. You're my wife now. There will never be anything between us."

I wasn't even worrying about getting pregnant. I probably should've been, but that's the last thing on my mind as I admit, "Is that what you tell all the girls so they don't make you wrap up?"

Link cages his arms around me, bracing his hands on the sink. "Other girls? There aren't any other girls."

I'd hope not. Otherwise, it's fucked up that he made me marry him. I'll be his wife, but I didn't sign up to act the part while he keeps his mistresses, and I made sure to tell him that on our way to the judge's house. It was the only thing I asked before I married him, and Link smirked at me as he said, "Of course."

In the mirror, I see he's wearing the same expression now as he did in the back seat of the car. Like something's funny, or it's a joke I just don't understand.

I'm serious. "I'm not talking about now. I mean—"

"I know what you mean. There aren't any other girls," he says, and I have to bite down on my lip to stifle my scream when he lets go of the sink and drops his hands to my hips, pulling me back the same time as he pushes forward, "not for fifteen years."

I had to have heard him wrong. The sensation of being stuffed full of him, the stretch, the ache, the delicious pain of having his thick cock trapping me between his hard chest and the sink in front of me... I had to have heard him wrong. No way did the Devil of Springfield admit that he hasn't been with another woman since *me*?

And if he did? Maybe he's referring to serious relationships, like what we once had. Knowing Link like I did, he couldn't have gone *fifteen years* without sex... could he?

I don't know, but the man behind me is fucking me like he has. Leaving one big hand as a brand on my hip, the other moves to my lower belly, keeping me with him so that I have no choice but to lean forward and ride his dick, matching the frantic pace he's started with.

"I did my time waiting," he pants, digging his fingers into my skin, holding me in place while he pounds into me. I cling to the sink for dear life, watching the dark look on his face in the mirror. "I did my penance. Now you're mine, Ava, and I fucking dare anyone to try to take you away from me."

I can't say anything to that, and not only because I'm breathing so heavily, I can't get a single word out. It's like someone's flipped a switch in him, and the cold, calculating gangster who thought it was a good idea to make me his wife because he needed one is replaced by a demanding beast whose expression says he's happy to devour me whole.

Marriage of convenience, I think to myself,

scraping the sink with my nails as everything—his possessive hold, the idea that anyone passing by the bathroom knows exactly what we're doing in here, his pace, my *need*—leads me toward a climax of my own... despite him telling me this would be a real marriage, I walked into the judge's house believing it was a marriage of convenience so that Link could keep his spot as the head of the Sinners Syndicate.

And maybe it is. A dangerous man like this doesn't need to be in love to fuck like he's obsessed. He doesn't need to feel affection to take a wife, and whatever he means by "waiting" and "penance", it doesn't matter.

I'm his, and as he grunts out his release, purposely yanking my ass toward him so that he comes as deep inside of me as he can before I get the chance to come myself, I tell myself that I have to remember that.

I belong to Devil, 'til death do us part.

the life

Mrs. Crewes

NINE
MRS. CREWES

AVA

I wake up with my head cradled in Link's lap.

That's not really a surprise. As soon as he ushered me back into his car, he spread his legs and instructed me to stretch out along the back seat, laying my head against his crotch.

For a second, I froze, believing that he expected me to down on him. I mean, after what just passed between us in the bathroom, I've accepted that acting like his wife "in all ways" basically means that I'm expected to fuck him whenever he wants until he eventually knocks me up.

So a blow job in the back seat of his fancy car? It seemed a reasonable conclusion to me, though I should've known better. If the Devil wanted me to suck his cock, he would've pulled it out and told me to do it.

He didn't. Instead, he ordered me to rest. It's not a long drive from the judge's house to where Link lives—wherever that is—but I was already yawning as he wrapped his arm around my shoulder, guiding me back to the car.

Once I listen and lay my head in his lap, I'm completely out. It's way too late for me, my sleepy time tea has me dozing, the adrenaline crash makes me feel like my arms weigh a hundred pounds each, and after the way Link demanded that orgasm from me, I'm *exhausted.*

There's no reason I should've woken up. If I hadn't, I probably would've slept straight through the night, though being that vulnerable around this new version of Link is a bad, bad idea.

I get an immediate reminder of that when I come to and the first thing I realize is that he's hard beneath me. I can feel his erection, hard and hot, through his suit pants, pushing against my cheek. After we finished in the bathroom, he tucked himself into his boxer briefs before zipping himself back up, then patting my dress back into place.

I have no idea what happened to my panties. Part of me hopes like hell that they're not lying in the middle of Judge Callihan's bathroom floor; if anything, maybe they got kicked aside and his cleaning lady will find them behind the toilet. The other part is intimately aware of the stickiness between my thighs, and the tangible proof that Link is more than ready to have sex with me again.

Closing my eyes again, hoping he didn't notice I woke up, I will myself into falling back asleep. Not like that would stop him. A few years into our sexual relationship, both Link and I began to explore our individual kinks. Though no one who looked at sweet-faced, adorable Ms. Monroe would ever think she had a thing for having sex where anyone could catch them—like, oh, fucking in the bathroom of someone else's home—Link's was on the opposite side of the spectrum.

He had a thing about fucking me when I was asleep. We would be in the same bed, me snoring away on my side, and the thought of taking me while I was unaware did something to him. As a nineteen-year-old, he seemed almost ashamed of it, and he never tried anything without getting my explicit consent back then.

So I gave it. If he had no problem letting me climb on his lap while we were at the movies, or draping a towel over my head so that I could blow him at the beach, why wouldn't I let him explore what turned him on the most? It's not like I ever told him no whenever he wanted sex back then, and I promised him that he had my permission to fuck me whenever he wanted, whether I was awake or not.

It actually worked out better for me. If he got a hard-on in the middle of the night, he could take care of it himself without waking me up for a quickie. I got uninterrupted sleep, he got off, and we were both happy—until he walked out on me, of course.

Now, fifteen years later, Link is acting like he still has my permission to just shove his dick inside of me whenever he wants.

And, well, he does, doesn't he? From the moment I said 'I do' and signed my name on our marriage license, I'm his...

For life, he said. 'Til death do us part, and all because I killed a man tonight.

As that thought races through my mind, the reminder banishing the last of my slumber, Link shifts in his seat. His palm runs over the top of my head, stroking my hair. It's a gentle caress at odds with how hard he took me in the bathroom, and I'm not so sure how to reconcile this side of Link with the boy I knew.

Then he murmurs, "Rise and shine, pet. We're home," and I stop worrying about it.

Oh, no. I have something else to focus on now.

After pulling myself up into a sitting position, I peer out of the tinted window and swallow roughly.

Now, I knew I wouldn't be returning to my house. As quick as our impromptu wedding was, it's barely been three hours since the phone call that changed my life. Is that enough time for a bunch of gangsters to "take care" of Joey's corpse and the blood spattered all over my carpet? I doubt it, and I figured I wouldn't go to *my* home.

This must be Link's, and since I'm his wife now, I guess it's mine, too.

"Oh." I almost crawl into Link's lap, trying to get a peek at the building we've pulled up at. "You live here?"

He rests his hand possessively on my ass. "We do," he says, proving me right. "The penthouse is ours."

The Paradise Suites North in Springfield is the tallest building in the city. Visitors might think it's a fancy hotel, and they're not wrong. The bottom half boasts rooms for the night that cost half as much as my mortgage, while the top is made up of luxury apartments for the well-to-do who pretend parts of Springfield—specifically the East End and West Side—aren't a dark, dangerous underworld.

And Link, one of the most dangerous of all according to his reputation, owns the *penthouse*.

Before I can say anything to that, someone opens his door. Beneath the glow of lights that illuminate the building no matter what time it is, I see a man a couple of years younger than me. He's good-looking in a slick sort of way, with styled blond hair, icy blue eyes, and a dimple in his left cheek as he grins down at us. Like Link, he's in a suit, though his is better tailored to his leaner frame.

"Been waiting for you, boss."

"Is everything ready inside?"

He nods.

Link hasn't moved his hand from my ass. With his

friend watching us closely, he squeezes me. "Let me introduce you to my underboss, pet. This is Royce McIntyre, second of all Sinners."

He smiles at me, a hint of a flirting tease there when he says, "You can call me 'Rolls'."

"She'll call you Royce," Link says firmly. "And if you don't stop flirting with my wife, you'll refer to her as Mrs. Crewes until you get it through your fucking skull that Ava is mine."

Oh my God. For years, I wanted nothing more than for him to claim me, but not like this. Not when I traded my hand for his protection, or when I'm his last option to have a kid before the syndicate decides he shouldn't lead them any longer.

Looking at Royce, I can't imagine him ever turning on Link. His entire expression changed when Link snapped at him, and while he still exudes a friendly manner, all flirtatiousness disappears instantly.

"You should've warned me. I didn't know this was Ava."

Link snorts. "The wedding dress didn't give it away?" He pats my ass this time, and if I wasn't afraid of offending him in front of his second, I would've sat down on the seat so he'd stop touching me like he owns me. I know he does, but still... "Royce is the one who brought it over for you. The ring, too."

Am I supposed to thank him for helping Link force me into marrying him? Sure, I agree, but it's not like I had any other choice—and considering he was probably there to help with "clean-up", he knows exactly why.

I don't thank him, though I do wave shyly over at him.

Link nods in approval at my greeting. Finally, he drops his hand, but only because he slides out of the car. With a gesture, he motions for me to do the same.

Grabbing the skirt on my dress, I shuffle my way out.

"Royce is going to bring you upstairs," Link tells me. "And your bags," he adds, and though he wasn't addressing the other man, Royce immediately heads over to the trunk where the driver threw my luggage inside. Once he's out of sight, Link lifts his hand, running his thumb along the edge of my jaw. "Be a good girl for him, okay?"

"You're leaving?"

"I have a couple of things to take care of. I'll be back soon."

I don't know how I feel about that. He was the one so quick to make me marry him tonight, and then we couldn't leave the judge's house until we consummated the marriage—which, unless Link's lost his stamina over the years, was also a lot quicker than it should've been.

However, now that he has me wearing his ring, he's even quicker to pass me off to his friend.

I shouldn't be hurt by that. Odds are that, whatever business he has, it's him holding up his end of our bargain. I married him, so now he has to make it so that no one knows what happened at my house tonight.

I nod. "Okay. I guess I'll see you later."

His hand is still on my jaw. Tightening his grip, he holds my head in place as he bends his down to mine. His kiss is bruising, almost punishing as he presses our lips together. Instead of coaxing mine to part, he forces his way into my mouth, devouring me whole.

I can't escape him. There is no relief, and as I reach out, fisting his button-down shirt, I cling to Link as he takes everything he wants from me.

When he finally releases me, I have a death grip on his shirt that takes a few seconds for me to break. I'm panting, not sure if I hate him for treating me like he owns me, or that I'm already addicted to this forceful, powerful side of him.

His eyes are blazing with an emotion I can't quite read as he threads his fingers in my hair, resting his chin on top of my head. With our height difference, it's probably the most comfortable for him—or it's just his way of showing me that he's in control.

I'm panting, but he sounds as cold as ice even as his words burn me up from the inside: "It's our wedding night, pet. The beginning of forever. I wouldn't miss a minute of it unless I had to. Remember that."

Catching my breath, resisting the urge to fall against his hard chest, I whisper, "I will."

AVA

"Ava, kochanie. I can't believe it's you!"

The moment I follow Royce and my two packed bags off of the private elevator that led us to the penthouse, I'm immediately engulfed in a tight hug that would've scared me shitless if I hadn't recognized the accented voice calling out to me a second before I was being squeezed.

Mona Jankowski was the building's grandmother when we were kids. She immigrated from Poland during her early twenties, settling in Springfield where she buried two husbands, three kids, and was still the sweetest old lady I've ever known.

Growing up, her apartment was a floor below my family's, right next door to the Crewes's. Because I spent all of my time there, she treated me like I was another one of her treasured grandchildren, but I haven't seen her since the day Link's mom kicked him out, and I left with him.

She always smelled like flour, I remember, breathing the same scent in now as she gives me an excited squeeze before letting me go.

Her grey hair is done up in curlers. Her big, fluffy body is covered by a white terrycloth robe, the hem of her pale pink nightgown escaping the bottom of it. Despite the late hour—and the fact that she must've been sleeping earlier—her rich brow eyes are alert, and her thin lips are spread in a big smile as she looks over at me.

She's aged a little in the fifteen years since I've seen her last, but I recognize her regardless.

"Mama Mona," I say, greeting her with the name all of us kids had for her back then, "what are you doing here?"

To be honest, I would've thought she'd pass by now. As a kid, she seemed so old, though now that I'm looking at her, I can't imagine that she's more than seventy, and still in good health if her rosy cheeks and big belly are any clue.

"I work for Mr. Lincoln," she says, beaming over at me. "He hired me as his... how do you say? In Polish, it's gosposia..." She snaps her fingers. "Housekeeper, that's it. I'm his housekeeper. He gave me a job when I needed one, and I get to take care of one of my chidrens."

I don't know how to respond to that. Did... did Link move Mama Mona out of the ramshackle apartments we grew up in once he made it big, letting her move in with him, hiring her as his housekeeper, taking care of her the same way she thinks she's doing him?

I glance past her, getting my first glimpse of the penthouse. It's a long hall, with a huge kitchen to my right, an elaborate living room to my left, and who knows what at the other end of the shadowed hall.

Looking back at Mona, I say, "You live here?"

THE DEVIL'S BARGAIN

"Tak. I was sleeping, but when Mr. Royce woke me up, telling me to get Mr. Lincoln's room ready for his new bride, I thought I was dreaming. O mój Boże, to see you here... I must still be. Tell me, Ava, are you the bride?"

This time, I glance down at the white dress I tugged on what feels like a lifetime ago now, glad that she can't see how wrinkled the skirt is behind me from where Link tossed it up and pounded away inside of me barely an hour ago.

With a half smile, I admit, "I am."

"My heart," Mona says, clutching her massive boob. "I thought one day I'd see you with Mr. Lincoln again, but today God blesses this home, bringing you back to us. Hura, hura."

Hura... whenever Mona was excited, she would say 'hura', an old-fashioned way of saying 'yay' or 'hooray' in Polish.

Well, at least one of us is happy about this situation...

A few steps to the side, Royce clears his throat. "She needs to go to sleep, Mona. Maybe you two can catch up in the morning?"

"Ach, yes, kochanie. You must be so tired. Come. Let us bring you to Mr. Lincoln's bedroom."

I gulp. Right. Because I'm his wife, so obviously I'd sleep in his bed.

Mona goes first, stomping her way happily forward in her matching slippers. I tiptoe behind her, my flats scraping against the hard floor. Royce brings up the rear, still carrying my two suitcases with him.

She stops at the first door on the right. It's closed, but when she pushes it open and flicks the switch just inside of the room, I see that it's a bedroom three times as big as mine back home.

The massive bed in the middle—a King, at least—is just as intimidating.

He has a dark oak headboard, and a bed frame that matches. All of the furniture is the same shade of brown. His sheets are a dark blue, the only spot of color in the whole space. It's definitely a man's bedroom, without any hint of femininity in there.

Maybe that's why I can't bring myself to walk in there.

That, or because all I'm thinking about are the countless other women who stood right where I am, knowing that Link might fuck them in there, but they'll never truly belong...

As if he can sense where my thoughts have gone, Royce sidles up next to me as Mona moves further into the room, patting the pristine sheets of the made-up bed. He's careful to keep at least a good two feet between us, but he still tilts his head toward me as he says, "How's it feel to be the first woman besides Mona to set foot in this room?"

My head snaps over at him. "What?"

Royce grins. "Don't worry. She's just his housekeeper. She makes the bed, she doesn't lie in it."

That's not what I meant.

Mona looks back at us. "Come in. Set her things down, Mr. Royce. I'll put them away for you in the morning, Ms. Ava—"

"It's just Ava, Mama Mona," I murmur.

She continues as if she hasn't heard me. "—but you should get some rest. I'll send Mr. Lincoln to you when he's home again."

So I get to rest in his big bed without him, and Mona will wait up to report to him after being interrupted from her own sleep earlier.

"I'll go to bed, but only if you do, too," I tell her. "Link can find his own way to bed."

And when he does, I'm not going to be there.

I... I can't.

While Mona nods her head, agreeing with whatever I say, I twist the wedding band Link slipped on my ring finger. It's at least two sizes too big for me, and I can't help but wonder who the dress and ring were meant for before me. Both Link and Royce made it obvious that he hasn't been jumping from relationship to relationship—that his empire comes first—but... I don't know. I can't believe a man as powerful, rich, and *gorgeous* as Lincoln Crewes is would stay purposely single, no matter how dangerous and busy he is.

Unless he has another reason why he did. He said that he only wanted to enter into this marriage of convenience—sorry, *real* marriage—because his syndicate expected him to take a wife. It didn't matter what the woman thought so long as he did what he was supposed to as the head of his crew.

I'm not his wife. No matter what he says, or who he tells that I am, I'm just the woman he needs to keep his position as head Sinner.

He's never let a woman into his bedroom? Why should he start now?

"Mama Mona," I ask, keeping my flats planted firmly in the hall even as she bustles around, telling Royce where to set down my luggage. "Does Link have any guest rooms in the penthouse?"

She stops, blinks, visibly confused. "Tak. Of course. Sometimes one of the boys stays, like Mr. Royce, and he asks me to keep them ready just in case. But they're empty tonight."

Perfect.

"Tonight, they won't be. I'll take my suitcases then," I tell Royce. "Point me in the direction of the nearest one, and I'll get myself settled in, if that's okay."

Mona starts fussing—I'm betting she's going to insist I stay in Link's room—but, surprisingly, Royce comes to my rescue.

Grabbing a suitcase in each hand, he offers me an undeniably amused grin. "Don't worry, Mona. I'll show the new Mrs. Crewes where to go."

She hesitates for a moment before her apple cheeks crease into a warm smile. "Of course, Mr. Royce. And I'll go prepare Ms. Ava some tea."

the life

Mrs. Crewes

TEN
CONNECTION

LINCOLN

My bed is empty.

On any other night, that's just what I would expect. But it's not any other night. It's my wedding night, and I'm missing my bride.

It's closing in on five in the morning. I'm exhausted and I'm horny, and the only thing that got me through reports from the clean-up crew and a recap from Burns was the promise of returning to the penthouse and finding Ava Monroe curled up in my bed.

I know she made it upstairs to the penthouse. Before Mona turned in again for the night, she assured me that Ms. Ava was settled in, and Royce said the same before I relieved him and my second shot straight for the elevator.

He was smirking as he left, but I'm used to that from Royce. I didn't even think about what he could've found so fucking funny, but as I walk into my bedroom and find the sheets not even mussed, I almost turn around and go after the prick. He must've known things didn't go according to plan—I explicitly gave orders that Ava was to be moved right into my personal space—and got the hell out before I found out.

I want to drag Royce by the collar to explain himself, but I want my wife even more.

There's no sign she even stopped in this room. The living room was empty, too, and when I throw open the bathroom door, she isn't in there, either.

Where the fuck did she go?

I don't know, but if I have to search the penthouse inch by inch to track her down, I will. She couldn't escape my watching eye when she was living her life out in Springfield. She hasn't got a prayer of escaping me on my territory.

If I'd been thinking rationally, I would have gone straight to the guest rooms. Since I wasn't, it takes me four rooms before I open a door and find my Ava curled up in the middle of the guest bed, pretty brown hair spilled on the pillow, curvy body covered up by an oversized t-shirt with enough leg on display that my cock twitches.

I've been hard all fucking night. Taking her once in the bathroom—consummating our marriage—had done nothing to take the edge off of fifteen years of need, and I only added to my penance when I let her lay her head in my lap, centimeters away from my erection without tugging on the zipper and slipping the crown between her lips.

I would've killed to do that. Only knowing that I had to uphold my end of our bargain before I could enjoy my new wife kept me sitting still in the car, stroking her hair, fantasizing about making her mine again and again.

I did what I could for tonight. Burns made sure that he was the car called to check out "suspected gunshots" in Ava's neighborhood, and my guys have already disposed of Maglione's body. His car is already in a chop shop on the West Side, and by tonight, its parts will be scattered.

Her house is cleaned, and I've got two of my best soldiers packing it up so that she'll be moved into mine in no time. Just like I promised, it's like tonight never happened.

At least, the part where Ava was forced to kill her ex to save herself. The part where she promised herself to me?

That definitely happened, and if she wants to pretend it didn't... I'll be happy to remind her.

She's snuffling, fast asleep, and when I call her name, she doesn't react. The Ava I knew was a light sleeper unless she had a little help, and I glance around the room, squinting into the shadows.

There's a mug sitting on the nightstand beside the bed.

I pick it up. It's half empty. Taking a sniff, I nod to myself when I catch a tiny whiff of the tasteless sedative I had Royce slip inside of the tea. Mona would've brewed her some on my orders, but despite the powder being tasteless, it has a faint nutty scent that I recognize over the floral tea.

Between how tired Ava must have been and the added boost from the sedative, she's dead to the world. Her luggage is on the floor, next to the guest room bed. One of the suitcases is partly open—probably from when she traded the wedding dress for her sleep shirt—and I kick it out of my way.

My wife belongs in my bed. It's as simple as that. No matter why she thought she'd get away with spending the night in one of my guest rooms, she better get used to the idea that, every morning from now on, she'll wake up next to me.

Slipping one hand under her thighs, the other under her back, I heft Ava up in my arms. Her weight is nothing to me, and I smile to myself as I carry her sleeping body out of this room and into mine. It's a bridal-style hold, and by the time I'm crossing the threshold with my new wife, I can't wait to get inside of her again.

I spread her out in the middle of the bed. Quickly shucking my clothes off, I give my hard cock a few quick strokes, trembling with the desire running through me.

This woman is mine. She always has been, and now that she has my ring on her finger, I couldn't care less about who touched her when I couldn't. I earned this—and if I didn't, I'm taking it anyway—and I'm not waiting until she's awake again to enjoy my wife again.

I don't undress her; to me, it's fucking hot for me to be completely naked while Ava keeps her shirt on. She didn't bother pulling on shorts—as though she remembered what being with me was like and expected that I'd find my way between her legs again as soon as possible—though I growl under my breath when I shove her shirt up and see that she's wearing panties again.

Her pair from earlier tonight is in my pants pocket. I took them after I fucked her in the bathroom at Callihan's house, a prize and a trophy in one. I loved the idea of her going bare after we finished, my come slipping out of her pussy, and her hole waiting just for me. I even used the silky panties to rub one out in my personal bathroom at the Playground tonight, when the urge to find her and fuck her got so bad that I had to make do with my fist.

I went fifteen years without working my cock into a hot cunt. Within hours, I started fiending, desperate to get inside of Ava again. It was like returning home when I bent her over the sink, forcing her to watch me as I made her mine. If I could've stayed there, I would've, but now that I can... I *will*.

The panties have to go, though. Grabbing the band, I work them down her body, breathing in deep when I reveal her sweet little pussy. I want to bury my face in her curls, lapping at her slit, swallowing her whole, but while I'd get pleasure out of that, my sleeping beauty would miss out on me tasting her again.

Later, I promise, slipping my hand between her thighs, pushing them apart. For now, I have something else I'm dying to do.

I trace her slit with my thumb, checking to see how dry she is. I'd never risk hurting her by fucking her when she wasn't ready, and I suck my thumb into my mouth, using some of my saliva to add some moisture. It's still not enough.

Fuck.

I don't have any lube. I haven't needed it, and I'm not about to use lotion and risk giving Ava any kind of infection because I was too desperate to fuck her without thinking of her safety.

That's not going to stop me, though. Grabbing her thighs, I position her right beneath my mouth and spit. Rubbing it into her pussy, it provides enough slipperiness that her body starts to lubricate itself. Dipping my finger inside her tight snatch, she sucks me in up to my knuckle.

Much better.

I spit on my hand next, using the precome beading

at the tip of my cock to get myself nice and slick for her. Once I'm as ready as I'm going to get, I push Ava on her side so that my big body can cocoon hers before I start feeding my cock into her pussy.

I'm only halfway seated when I can't stop myself from moaning her name. "Ava, fucking *Ava*."

She doesn't stir, and I push a little more, taking my time, enjoying her tight grip as I squeeze her hip, pulling her slumbering body up against my bare chest.

Only when my dick is as far inside as it can go do I curve my arm around her, trapping her in my embrace. I pump a few times, enough to send shivers of pleasure through me, before throwing my leg over hers, keeping us connected with my cock nestled inside of her.

Holding her like this... claiming her as intimately as I can... it's not about me just getting off tonight. Not really. If I wanted a tight hole and a quick nut, I could get a fleshlight, and it would be similar to shoving my cock inside of a sleeping woman just to feel her squeezing my length.

For me, it's always been about the connection and feeding the possessiveness inside of me. And not just with any partner, but Ava in particular. Just like how she's the only woman I've ever fucked, she's the only one I've ever fantasized about being connected to in every way that matters.

The first time she gave me consent to fuck her from behind while she was sleeping, I was so excited about getting to try my kink out that I didn't even have to thrust. Just knowing my Ava trusted me enough to own her body when she was completely vulnerable had me shooting my load almost instantly.

I got better, though, to the point that I could go for hours so long as I didn't move. That's when I realized that, as much as I loved fucking her while she slept, I got even more pleasure out of slipping my cock inside of her and just keeping it there.

That's what I'm doing now. Eventually, I'll lose control and I'll thrust until I've filled her up with my come, but I just need to hold her. To touch her. To enjoy the feel of her in my arms and her heat scalding my cock.

I lose track of how long I've warmed myself up with her body. I don't sleep because I'm fucking terrified that I'll wake up and discover that this has all been a dream. To Ava, no doubt she's convinced she's living a nightmare, but I've done everything I could for a second chance with this woman.

And now I have it.

Because I'm still awake, I can tell when Ava starts coming around—and when she realizes that I've pinned her to me, and she has my cock inside of her.

Her body stiffens a second before she tries to move away from me. I gasp at how her movement jostles my cock, and she whimpers as it hits her that she's not going anywhere.

"It's me," I whisper. "It's your husband."

If I live to be a hundred, I'll never forget the thrill

that roars through me the first time I call myself Ava's husband—or the way she murmurs *Link* in the early morning light.

Ah. She knows exactly who's inside of her now.

I roll my hips, dragging my cock halfway out of her before nestling myself inside my wife again. "That's right, pet. You're right where you belong."

the life

Mrs. Crewes

ELEVEN
SPITFIRE

LINCOLN

"Where... uh... where am I?"

Look at that. Moving with me, almost as though her body craves mine as much as I do hers, she doesn't say anything about the way I'm slowly fucking her. Oh, no. She just wants to know why she's not in the room she remembers falling asleep in.

"Our room," I tell her, punctuating *our* with a harder thrust that has her nails digging into my arm. "That's part of being married, pet. We share a bed."

With our bodies intertwined, I feel it when she gulps, then says softly, "And this? Waking up to your dick inside of me? Is that part of being married, too?"

Of course it is. She gave me permission when we

were young adults, and as far as I'm concerned, she only reinforced it when she agreed to marry me.

I'll fuck her when I want. Kiss her when I want. Love her when I want... and I'll do whatever it takes to make her love me again.

Starting with reminding her just how much I own her and her body.

"Don't forget, pet," I murmur, bending my head and suckling on her neck. Her back arches out, squeezing me again, leading me to moan before I tell her in a ragged voice, "I own you."

She stiffens again, her body so tight that my cock feels like she has it in a vice. A jolt of pleasure slams into me, and I know that, if she does that again, I won't be able to hold back my orgasm. I'm not done playing with her, so I grit my teeth, holding on—

—and then she whispers into the room, "Is that how it is?," in a small voice, and I stop worrying about going off sooner than I want to. To hear Ava sound as hurt like that... fuck, I might just lose my erection entirely.

I thought she was playing along with me. Was I wrong?

I shift my hips, giving her a tentative pump. "It's what you agreed to," I remind both of us.

She's quiet for a moment, but she doesn't try to pull away from me. The opposite, actually. While I pump again, building a slow rhythm now that she's awake, she scoots back, her ass pushing back against my lower belly.

She's so fucking soft. Just that added connection has me moaning softly, and I drop my hand, grabbing the cheek nearest to me. Kneading the flesh, I pump faster, and while I plan on going back to warming my cock inside of her heat once I get her off—and me, too, at this rate—if I don't come inside of this woman right now, I might just die.

For a moment, I think she's got the same idea. Ava is moving with me, rocking back as I tilt my hips again, slamming myself to the hilt inside of her like her soft body was made for my hard one. She lets out a gasp that is music to my ears, and I grunt her name as I move my hand in front of her, searching for her clit so that I can make her come first.

I slide my fingers through her damp curls, but before I can find her clit, she slaps my hand.

And then, in a stronger voice than before, she says, "You know what, Link? You're right. And I said I'd be your wife in all ways, didn't I?" Too stunned by the sudden change in her to realize what she's doing, Ava pulls away from me, letting my erection slide right out of her pussy.

We're not separated for long. Wrapping her hand around my slick cock, squeezing me with her fingers to the point that my eyes almost roll to the back of my head, she uses her other hand to push me onto my back.

If I didn't want to move, I wouldn't have. But, eager to see what she's planning, I let her knock me onto my back—and I'm rewarded with Ava shoving her night shirt high enough to reveal her delectable little pussy to me before she throws one leg over me, positioning her cunt right over the head of my cock.

"You think sex is all there is to being married. Fine. Then let me fuck you, *husband*."

And, as she spits out the word *husband*, Ava sinks down on top of my cock.

"Fuck me," I breathe out. "Oh, pet... do whatever the fuck you want to me. Fuck me, kiss me, take a knife from the kitchen and stab me in my God damn heart if you want, but, for fuck's sake, do it now."

"Oh, Link... I *will*."

Bracing her soft hands on my scarred, tatted chest, she starts to ride me. I almost want to close my eyes just to enjoy the sensations of Ava working my body in a way I haven't experienced in so damn long, but that would mean taking my eyes off of her for a split second and I can't even do that.

Her hair falling forward, hiding the determined expression twisting her gorgeous features, she's moving back and forth, rocking again, then lifting herself up, dropping down on top of me, doing everything and anything to show that I just don't own her.

She owns *me*—and she always has.

I fucking love it almost as much as I love her. I've never stopped, and as I feel my sac tightening, Ava about to wring my come right out of me, I admit that this is the Ava who tried to stop me from walking away. The spitfire with the unholy temper.

The woman I've obsessed over for fifteen fucking years and who I might not deserve, but who I'm going to keep anyway.

Especially when she squeezes me so damn tightly that I couldn't keep myself from coming if one of my enemies had a gun to my head.

"There." Her green eyes glitter wickedly in the moonlight. "You want an heir so damn bad? Maybe that time did the trick."

Is that what she was trying to do? Using sex against me instead of as a way to remember how close we once were—how close we're going to be from now on—and then throwing my own words back in my face?

Because they *are* my words, aren't they?

Chest heaving, fingers curling into the sheets so that I don't dig into her pretty skin, leaving bruises as a mark of just how much I want this woman, I realize that I fucked up. I probably did in more ways than I can count—starting with blackmailing her into giving me forever when I would've helped her just because she called me—but as Ava starts to climb off of me without chasing an orgasm of her own, I know that fucked up big time.

I can't believe I let her think for a single second that the only reason I want to fuck her is because she's a wet pussy and an empty womb and not because she's starred in every single fantasy I've had since I was twelve years old.

I finally convinced her to let me touch her when we were fifteen. At sixteen, we had awkward sex for the first time. By nineteen, I was sure I would never want to fuck anyone else—and when I started my penance at twenty, I told myself I never would.

It's always been Ava Monroe for me, or no one. And now, fifteen years later, I have her back in my bed... and maybe I had to carry her there first, but there's no way in hell I'm letting her leave it without her being satisfied first.

Fuck. I don't plan on letting her leave it at all, but I don't need an excuse to pleasure this woman.

Gonna take it anyway, though.

As Ava starts to move away from me, I clasp my hands on her waist, grumbling to myself when her sleep shirt gets in the way of my palms touching her, skin to skin. I want to rip it off of her, but there's only so far I want to push Ava tonight, and from the way fire seems to flash in her eyes as I trap her on top of me, I think I passed it already.

Oh, well.

In one quick move, I tilt her to her back, cradling her in the gap left between my legs when I spread them to make room for her. Once I have her trapped there, I shift my position so that she's splayed out, her ankles are hooked over my shoulders, and my mouth is hovering inches over her pussy.

As I shove her shirt up high enough that I can see her tits as I drop my chin to my sweat-damp sheet, she finally stammers out, "What are you doing?"

Isn't it obvious?

"Licking you clean, pet." Curling my tongue, I dip the point inside of her pussy, gathering as much of my come as I can. Mingled with Ava's taste, I can pretend I'm not swallowing my own spunk, but if this is what I have to do to get my point across, I'll do it.

Maybe then my new bride will understand there isn't anything I won't do for *her*.

I thought it was obvious, but she doesn't seem to understand. "Why? Why would you do that?"

I hate to have to lift my head from her damp curls and the heat of her pussy, but I do long enough to meet her perplexed gaze.

"You think I'm only in this to knock you up. If it happens, it happens, but forgive me if I want to enjoy my wife for longer than a couple of months before I have to share her with someone else."

I waited fifteen years for another chance with Ava. As much as it has my dick stirring, going hard again to think of this woman swelled up with my kid inside of her, I wasn't kidding when I said I plan on enjoying her as much as I can.

It's been one night, and I'm already fucking addicted. And that's only if I pretend I already *wasn't*.

I know this is just performative. Licking my come out of her while also nuzzling her clit with my nose, sucking her labia into my mouth, doing everything and anything to make her come on my face... my tongue is powerful enough to have her panting, writhing as she rubs her pussy all over me, but it's nowhere near as long as my dick. I can't get every drop, but, fuck, I hope I made my point clear.

And when Ava shoves her fingers through my hair, shoving herself against me as though she could care fucking less if she suffocated me right now, I have to smile into her pussy as her legs start to shake, heels digging into my bare back.

Yeah. I think I did.

the life

Mrs. Crewes

TWELVE
THE PLAYGROUND

AVA

Link calls me his wife.

It doesn't take long before I realize that means I'm his *prisoner*.

Maybe I should have expected that. It's not like I agreed to marry some ordinary blue-collar guy. He's the head of a crime syndicate with enemies to match, and if it gets past his crew that I'm his wife, I'd be an easy target.

That's not counting how I got into this mess in the first place because I'd somehow caught Damien Libellula's attention. Link insisting that I stay in the penthouse isn't just his way of controlling me. I'd bartered my freedom for his protection and, well, this is it.

He'd deny that I was his prisoner. Technically, if I wanted to leave, I could, but the only condition is that I have to have someone with me. Of course, he wants that to be him. He's taking his role as my husband very seriously, from eating dinner with me each night, bringing me home a trinket every time he leaves me behind, and climbing into bed with me so that he can perform his husbandly duties by making me scream his name into the darkness.

That first night was a fluke. At least, when it comes to how he put chasing his own orgasm before making it good for me; him indulging in cockwarming after he bones me into sleep is a regular occurrence. He explained to me that he was so determined to consummate our marriage in the bathroom that he wasn't thinking about anything else, and he's more than made up for it. There hasn't been a single night since I moved into the penthouse that he doesn't focus on my pleasure. Alternating before rough and gentle, frantic and sweet, every time I see a glimpse of the boy I knew, it only hurts me even more when I remember this could've been us.

It could've been us all along, if he didn't put the life in front of a happily-ever-after with me.

He still does. Proof is in how much time he spends working on "business". He might slip into bed with me every night, but that's because it didn't take long for him to realize some of my quirks. When I went to bed —in his, because I learned my lesson about trying to put some distance between us—the second night, he didn't like that I fell asleep without him.

I had to explain that I was catching up on all the missed sleep from the night before. Besides, I'm not like him and his men. I don't do my business at night, and I'm happily in bed by ten. Link didn't say anything to that. He did, however, leave after dinner the next night only to return at quarter to ten so that he could take me to bed.

I was in bed by ten, but by the time Link was done with me, it was well after midnight when I curled up next to his sculpted body, tracing the elaborately-designed cross on his chest before I fell asleep. Hours later, I woke up to discover he was gone, and I tried not to let that sting.

He came home to me, but I've always heard that the Devil runs the night. Of course he would slip out to do whatever it is he does while I stay behind with whatever guard he posts in the penthouse with me.

A different guy is wandering around it whenever Link leaves. Glorified babysitting duty, I ruefully think of it. He was so annoyed when I asked if they were necessary that I decided not to bring it up again—though I do spend my first two weeks as Mrs. Crewes pretending they're not there.

There's one of them who tries to be a little friendly with me. About my age, with short black hair and deep brown eyes, Bobby—seriously, he introduces himself as *Bobby* despite being at least thirty-five, thirty-six—seems to warm up to me when he finds out that I'm a teacher. He has a niece starting kindergarten in my school district, and his girlfriend does something for the school. He brushes me off when I ask if I might know her, but at least he treats me like a person and not his boss's new pet.

Sometimes, I think he treats me with more consideration than *Link* does.

Do I use that against the soldier? I hate to admit it, but I totally do. Call it manipulative if you want, but I couldn't see any other way around it. Link was purposely keeping me separate from the syndicate part of his life, and it was driving me crazy.

I'm the one who asked if this is supposed to be a marriage of convenience. If he just wanted me to pretend to be his wife, I would force myself not to care what he was doing. He's the one who wants me to believe that this marriage is legit—so why is he hiding me away like I'm his dirty little secret?

If he's really my husband, I want to get to know Link. It's so hard for me to reconcile the rumors I've heard about the wicked Devil when I've only seen glimpses of his dark side. I almost *want* to think this version of Link is as bad as the stories make him out to be, because if he isn't? I might have been better off waiting for the cops to come after me for shooting Joey.

I'm not made for prison, but I... I just don't know if I'll be able to survive Lincoln Crewes breaking my heart again.

He thinks he's jealous. Of the two of us, co-dependent as we were once upon a time, I was always the worse one. He brawled for money. I got into slap fights when I saw some of the other girls who fawned over the fighters oohing and ah-ing over my Link.

Part of moving on meant I had to stop thinking about all the women he's loved after me. Sex, I could forgive, but if he loved someone else? I never did. Sure, I'd taken a few lovers over the years, and I almost married Brandon, but I never *loved* him. That's why I called off our wedding at the last minute. It didn't matter that Link walked out on me.

He's the only man I ever loved, and even if I don't know if I can love the man he's become, I have the chance to. Hearing him tell me that there's never been anyone after me—not a fling, not a one-night stand, and definitely no one else he admits to loving—has me halfway there.

Maybe I'm being naive, but I get the idea that, once he lets me into his entire life, we really can make this marriage work. And that's why, one evening after dinner, when he leaves to take care of "something", I point-blank ask Bobby where I can find Link if I need him.

Poor guy. He answers me before thinking, and I'm sure he'll regret it later, but that doesn't change a thing.

I have a name: The Devil's Playground, the infamous nightclub run by the Sinners Syndicate on the West Side that I've heard of, but never visited for fear of accidentally seeing Link and having him look right through me.

It should've been obvious. It's the Sinners' headquarters, so of course he would spend a lot of his time there. But once I have confirmation... I decide it might be time to visit my husband at work.

He won't be expecting me. Link never tells me where he goes when he leaves. He just says it's 'business' and leaves it at that.

Well, tonight I'll find out just what that means.

The Devil's Playground.

With a stylized, neon green devil with a pitchfork and a pointed tail underlining the name in a bright, glowing white, I'm a little intimidated as I walk down the sidewalk.

Suddenly, I feel very underdressed.

That's my fault. Knowing that I'm probably not supposed to leave the penthouse without telling anyone, I did anyway. I waited until Bobby disappeared into another room, taking a phone call, then ducked out why Mona was busy.

I googled the club on the elevator ride down, pleased to see it was only a ten-minute walk away. I pulled on my favorite sneakers just in case—after quickly rummaging through the packed boxes from my house that I haven't brought myself to undo just yet—and left wearing the short-sleeve shirt and jeans I was wearing today.

It never occurred to me that there would be a dress code for the club. Based on what the long line of people waiting along a rope stanchion has on? There is, and it's a lot more revealing, leathery, and tight than what I'm wearing.

Lucky for me, I have a golden ticket. I don't wait in the line—only because it looks like an hour's wait and somebody will notice I'm missing by then—instead heading right for the bouncer at the door. I'm not so sure if he'll believe me when I tell him that I'm Link's wife, but as though fortune herself is smiling down on me, one of my babysitters is stepping out with a date at the same time as I'm trying to explain who I am.

He's one of the ones who introduced himself. His name is Marco, and though he smirks when he sees me, he voices that I really am Mrs. Crewes. Despite the judging look the bouncer gives me—I choose to believe it's my outfit, and not *me* he's judging—he steps aside, letting me walk right in.

The atmosphere slams right into me, and my first impression is that I'm never going to find Link in here.

It's so crowded. Dark and crowded and *hot*, with bodies everywhere, most of them hidden in shadows, or bumping along, mimicking fucking on the dance floor. It smells of smoke and sweat, plus the overwhelming stink of booze, and my nose wrinkles.

That's not the only sense of mine that's affected. The music is so loud in here, I can feel the rhythm of it beneath the soles of my sneakers.

Figuring I'll get used to how overwhelming it is if I just immerse myself into the club, I grit my teeth, barely resisting the urge to clap my hands over my ears as I start to circle the place, searching for Link.

For a moment, I think about grabbing my phone and dialing his number. If he's here, it might be easier for him to find me, but it's so loud, I can't hear myself think, let alone have a conversation on the phone.

After about fifteen minutes, I realize that this is pointless. Not only do I not see Link anywhere, but I haven't passed a familiar face with the exception of the Sinner who I saw on his way out. You would think, in a club run by the syndicate, I'd recognize *someone*, but the fact that I don't just reinforces how much Link keeps me separate from this part of his life.

Honestly, I'm beginning to see why.

People are openly doing drugs on the floor. Before, when I thought the clubbers were mimicking fucking, I was wrong; some of them are literally doing just that in public. And those who want a little privacy? I've seen more than a few couples head upstairs where, I discover after scooting behind them and eavesdropping a little, the working girls in the club take their clients for an hour or two at a time.

I detour away from the stairs, though I won't lie and say that I don't stand on the edge of the dance floor, watching some of the couples fuck out in the open. I'm not usually a voyeur—I prefer to be the one getting watched, if I'm being honest—but there's something about this place that has me drawn to the dark, sadistic nature of the clubbers giving in to their need, swaying along to the music at the same time as they fuck.

It's mesmerizing, and I probably would've stood there long and stared if I didn't hear a female voice calling my name over the music.

"Ava? Holy shit, that can't be you."

I whip my head around.

The woman I'm facing is wearing one of the Devil's Playground uniforms: a skirt so short they're closer to being panties, and a cropped t-shirt with the logo on it that dips low enough to show off the lacy edge of her red bra. Her face is made-up expertly, showing off her light brown eyes, and her golden curls are arranged artfully around her face.

I've never seen her looking like this before, but I recognize her instantly.

Heidi Fox is a third-grade teacher at Springfield Elementary, and one of my co-workers. I'm used to seeing her fresh-faced in casual cotton dresses and... whoa. Seeing her like this? Excuse me for being so damn shocked.

Moving closer so that she can hear me over the music, I say her name in disbelief. "Heidi? What are you doing here?"

She gestures at her get-up. "Working, obviously. Waitressing."

"Really?"

"My boyfriend got me the job." She laughs, but despite her smile, there's not a drop of humor in it. "As if teachers don't get paid shit already, I needed the money during summer break. What about you? What are you doing at the Playground?"

Heidi's gaze runs over me, but there's such a marked difference between her waitressing uniform and what I'm wearing that it's obvious I don't belong.

Feeling like I've been put on the spot, I simply say, "I'm looking for my husband."

"You're married? When did that happen?" Her brow furrows. "Weren't you dating this mechanic guy last I heard? I thought you broke up."

I've never dated a mechanic. "Joey? He was in sales, and, yeah. We broke up."

"And you married him?"

I shake my head. "Um. No. I..." How to explain? The way her eyes are bugging out of her head so far, they might pop the rest of the way if I tell her I was blackmailed into marrying her boss—and that I killed Joey two weeks ago. "I reconnected with an old ex," I settle on. "One thing led to another and we eloped."

That's what you can call our whirlwind wedding, right?

"Wow. Congratulations." She pauses for a moment. "And you're happy?"

"Thanks. It all happened so fast, but yeah. I am." So far. "What about you and your boyfriend?"

Her eyes lit up. "Bobby's great."

Bobby…

Oh.

Well, look at that. I guess I know his girlfriend, after all.

"I'm glad to hear it. Good for you, Heidi."

"Thanks. He's got big plans for us." She gives me a conspiratorial smile. "Maybe we'll both have husbands by the time summer ends."

Heidi seems delighted by the prospect. Me? I can't even imagine what my life will be like by then. Will I even be going back to school? Link's made reference to the fact that I'll never have to work a day in my life again, and as heavy-handed as he was in moving me out of my house and into his, I wouldn't put it past him to suddenly decide that I'm quitting my job.

Of course, then he'll tell me it's too risky to teach first-graders, and that it's better if I stay in the penthouse…

Right. I don't know why he's so worried. He promised me that he would take care of the trouble I was in, and as far as I know, he has. He held up his end of our bargain, I'm doing mine by being his wife, and that's that—and I believe that up until the moment someone grabs my bicep from behind.

My immediate instinct is to pull away, but the grip is so bruisingly tight—and I'm so caught off guard—that my tug doesn't do anything to escape the hold.

There's only one man that I know who is strong enough to keep me where he wants me while also acting as though he can grab me whenever he wants. This is his club, too, and maybe I just missed his deep rumble as he calls me 'pet' over the loud music.

I stop struggling. No matter what kind of marriage we have, I agreed to act the part of Link's wife. He's the type of guy who would demand total loyalty and respect from his bride. Jumping and fighting him off when he approaches her on the dance floor... that might make the rest of the syndicate have questions about us.

Pulling a smile to my face, I turn my head so that I can show my husband just how happy I see him.

One problem, though.

That's not my husband.

the life

Mrs. Crewes

THIRTEEN
DEVIL

AVA

The man squeezes my upper arm as he lets out a low whistle. This close, I can't miss the sound, or when he chuckles to himself as he says, "I fucking love it when the face looks as good as the ass. This must be my lucky night."

I have no idea who he is. At least a head taller than me, with short black hair, a narrow face, dark eyes lit up with lust, and a crooked smile, he's definitely not Link. He's not as broad in the shoulder, or as muscular as Link is, though he's a lot bigger than I am.

No wonder I can't break free from his grip.

"Let go of me," I tell him, twisting my arm beneath his fingers.

"No way, sweetheart. I paid for a room upstairs, and you're just the girl I'm taking with me."

What?

Oh my God. Oh my *God*. This creep thinks that I... he thinks that I work here, like some of the other girls in this place.

Suddenly, Heidi's not-so-veiled comments about teachers not making enough money seems a whole lot clearer. I thought she meant that she was selling out, waitressing for a little extra cash. But that... that's not what she meant, was it?

The women who work upstairs don't just sell liquor and appetizers. They sell *themselves*—and this guy thinks that I'm also for sale.

I'm not going to judge them for what they do to survive. I'm not going to judge the women at Link's club if they sleep with these assholes because they want the money. But that's not my thing. Link's different, because he's *Link*, but I'm not going to let anyone else think that they can touch me without my permission.

I'm screwed, though. Glancing around, I see that Heidi is gone. She disappeared into the crowd, and I don't see anyone else that I recognize. Considering what kind of place this is, I doubt anyone even realizes that I'm two seconds away from freaking out.

I don't know what else to do. I think about screaming, but the music is loud—and I don't want to draw attention to myself if I don't have to. Link's obviously not here yet, either. I don't want to cause him any more trouble than I already have if he finds out about this.

This guy can be reasoned with, right? He's not just going to pick a girl off of the dance floor and drag her upstairs without her going along with it... *right*?

"I think you got the wrong idea. I don't work here."

For a split second, I think it works. He lets go of my bicep—but before I can move away from him, he grabs my wrist instead. Flipping my arm over, he smirks triumphantly when he sees that my forearm is bare. He switches wrists, doing the same to the other.

"You don't have Devil's mark on you. In here, that means you're up for grabs, baby, and you should've known that before you walked through the doors."

I definitely *didn't*.

"Besides, everyone has their price." He tightens his hold on my right wrist, starting to drag me away from the center of the dance floor. "Let's see how good you are and then we can talk about yours."

No!

"You can't do this," I gasp out. "I'm married. Look. I'm married and my husband—"

Throwing up my left hand, I go to show him my ring, my stomach twisting when I see that the oversized wedding band that Link slipped on my hand is missing.

The man smirks over his shoulder at me as I stare in horror at my naked ring finger. "Nice try, sweetheart. Even if you were married, that doesn't mean shit here. Half the guys banging the whores upstairs go home to their wives when they're done."

I'm barely listening to the sleaze in his tone. I'm too busy trying to figure out when and where the ring must have slipped off my finger. I had it this morning. I remember shoving it down to the webbing of my hand after I brushed my hair, and I swear I had it on when I was talking to Heidi—

"Come on. Time's ticking, and I plan on getting my money's worth to— *whoa*."

It all happens so fast. One second, he was pulling me toward the stairs that would lead to the second floor of Link's club. The next? Someone has grabbed him by the collar, so strong that they manage to rip his hand away from my wrist.

He yelps, and I spin around, trying to see who my savior is.

Chest heaving, eyes wild and fierce, his big hand firm on the collar of the other guy's shirt, is *Link*.

In the middle of the Devil's Playground, he looks bigger. Stronger. Darker.

Murderous.

For the first time since I called Link for help, I'm meeting Devil—and I'm frozen in place as he glares at the man in his grasp.

"Devil," he gasps.

"What the fuck do you think you're doing? Laying hands on my wife... do you want me to fucking kill you? Because I think I'm going to have to fucking kill you."

"She wasn't marked," the man starts to explain,

voice frantic and high as he realizes that, when I said I was married, *this* is my husband. "I thought she was fair game."

"Yeah?" Link twists his fist in the guy's shirt, lifting him a good two inches off the ground. "You thought wrong."

As my hands fly to my mouth, covering it as I watch in horror, Link takes a swing. The guy can't avoid the punch, and his head snaps over his shoulder as Link's fist connects with his face.

Blood sprays everywhere, but if I thought Link got his point across with one hit, I was *wrong*.

I've seen him fight before. It was how he made money for us when I was still scrimping and saving and trying to put myself through college, and I couldn't accept money from him without being there, supporting him during his back alley fights, mopping him up when he was on the losing end of a brawl.

He was always a hard hit. He didn't often lose, and even when he did, the other guy looked nearly as bad as he did.

Tonight? It is no contest. Link isn't fighting for the pot. He's whaling on the other guy for *honor* or some shit like that, and all I can do is whimper into my palm as he hits him again and again until he's hanging limply in his hold.

He's not dead. That's the only thing I can think of as Link drops him to the dance floor. The guy groans as he hits the ground, immediately trying to crawl away.

No one helps him. Whether it's because they don't want to get involved, or they know that Link is the Devil of Springfield and this is his place, I don't know. But not one soul offers to help the guy, and Link adds insult to injury by booting him one last time, getting him away from us.

And then he turns on me.

"Come here." He holds out his hand. "Ava, now."

I inch over to him, watching his hand move because it's better than staring into the face of the brawler that just beat the shit out of a guy for touching me.

It's dotted with blood. At first, I think it's the guy on the floor's blood— until Link gets antsy, flexing his fingers, gesturing for me to go to him and I see that his knuckles are split from the force of his hits. Some of the blood is his, and I don't know how I feel about that.

I do, however, go to put my hand in his.

I wasn't thinking. Still shocked by the brutality Link just showed off, I definitely wasn't thinking as I offer him my *left* hand.

Link snatches it, spreading my fingers apart so that it's obvious he's focusing on the fourth one.

His head snaps up, eyes locking on mine. "Where is it, Ava?"

He looks so angry, the words catch in my throat.

Thrusting my hand down, breaking the connection, Link looms in front of me. "You're my wife. You're *mine*. That ring proves it, and you took it off?"

"It fell off," I begin at last, trying to defend myself.

Link isn't having it. "You took it off, then you let some random fucker touch you."

Let him? "I was trying to get away—"

"You shouldn't have been here in the first place. You don't belong here, Ava," he tells me. No shit. His dark eyes are blazing at me, jaw clenched as he spits out, "If I wanted a whore for a wife, I would've married any of the waitresses Royce tried to hook me up with."

I go up on my tiptoes, going nose-to-nose with Link. "Maybe you should have."

He purses his lips. From the fury inherent in every line of his face, I know he's dying to continue our argument, and the old Link would have.

But this isn't the old Link I used to know. It isn't *my* Link.

This is the Devil of Springfield, and when his voice goes icy cold, sending shivers up and down my spine, I remember that as he says, "We'll discuss this later, pet."

I open my mouth. Link shakes out his hand, turning away from me. "Chance."

A guy materializes from out of the crowd. He's a tall dark-haired guy in his late twenties, give or take thanks to his baby face, and hero worship in his big brown eyes as he steps in front of Link.

"Yes, boss?"

"Bring my wife back to the penthouse." He pauses for a moment, and though I can't see his face, I can only imagine the expression on it. "And don't let her leave again."

"Link—"

Without turning around, he walks away from me.

I almost follow him. The last time I let him go like that, that was the end of us. I don't know what kind of 'us' we have now, but he seems determined to keep me—

"Come with me, Mrs. Crewes," Chance says. "I'll get you back to the boss's house."

—as a prisoner, just like I thought.

the life

Mrs. Crewes

FOURTEEN
LINCOLN

AVA

Chance relieves Bobby, taking over his post once we're back at the penthouse.

He seems nice enough, for a Sinner. He's definitely got a hard-on for Link, and he spends most of the ride back to Paradise Suites marveling over how much of a beatdown he gave the "wallet" back at the club. Having arrived right as Link did, Chance had a front-row seat to watching as Link's critical eyes roved over the entire club upon his entrance.

He saw me first, then the man who was yanking on my arm. It happened just as fast as I thought it did, with Link storming across the dance floor, pulling us apart so that he could beat the ever-loving hell out of the man for daring to touch his wife.

But that's the problem, I discover. Until Link

referred to me as his wife in front of Chance, he had no idea that the boss was married. He's not the first one, either. The men he sends to watch over me when he can't be in the penthouse... they all know, but it seems like my wonderful husband has decided to keep our wedding a secret from the rest of the Sinners Syndicate.

That doesn't make any sense to me. The whole point of me agreeing to marry him in exchange for his protection was that he needed a wife because his men expected him to have one.

But how does that work if none of them know we're married?

I don't want to think about it. Every time I do, I can't stop flashing back to the moment he snatched that man, and I saw murder written on his face. I honestly believe that, if I wasn't watching him beat that guy, he would've killed him. Everything happened in a flash, but I swear I remember him sparing me one look toward the end before he tossed the guy aside.

He was checking for my reaction, seeing how his wife liked seeing the Devil hard at work.

I *didn't,* and after the way he reacted when he saw that my wedding ring was missing, it's a good thing that he stayed behind in the club while sending me back home.

I don't expect Link to come back anytime soon. He was furious, I was in shock, and he probably has some more "business" to take care of. Me? I feel the need to hop in the shower to wash off the blood that spattered on me, and the memory of that creep's hand on my skin.

About an hour later, after I'm showered, dressed, and sitting in the living room, watching television while Chance hovers in the hallway, watching over me while I pretend he isn't, the doors open.

My head turns at the familiar *whoosh*, and I'm just in time to see Link walking into the room.

He's changed, too. Earlier, he was in wearing one of the suits he pulls on when he has a "business meeting" to attend. Now? He's traded it for a short-sleeved black top that stretches across his sculpted chest, black jeans, and boots. The blood is washed from his skin, and there's something shiny smeared on his knuckles.

Neosporin, maybe? Someone cleaned him up, and it wasn't me.

He's not alone, either, which is another reason to stay quiet as he moves to stand in front of the couch. It's not just that I feel a pang at knowing that, despite being moved into his house, I'm still nothing more than a fixture kept apart from his real life... only, yes, it is, and I look away from my fiercely beautiful husband, focusing on his companion, instead.

He's pretty. At least a decade younger than me and Link, he has shoulder-length black hair, delicate features, and light brown skin. His eyes are warm, his smile friendly, and apart from his face, every inch of skin I see on him is covered in tattoos in shades of black and grey.

He's carrying a large black case in one hand. With the other, he waves at me.

Link makes a rumbling noise in the back of his throat.

His friend drops his hand.

Okay, then.

Link points at the glass table next to the couch I'm lounging on. "You can set up there," he says, and the younger man nods.

Grabbing the table, he lifts it easily, shifting it so that's in front of me. Once he has, he pops open his case on one side of the rectangular table and starts unloading supplies.

Gloves, paper towels, a sealed needle, tiny plastic vials, ink—

"Cross does the inking for the syndicate," Link announces, just as the man—Cross—pulls on a pair of gloves and starts to assemble his tattooing machine. "I brought him here to give you a tat."

"What? Me?"

He nods. "I won't risk you losing another wedding band or taking it off when it suits you. My way, you have it permanently inked into your skin, and everyone will know that you're mine."

I blink. "Are you telling me that you're tattooing a *ring* on my finger?"

"Something like that." He nods at the side of the

table in front of me where Cross isn't setting his supplies out. "Lay your hand on the table, pet."

Not willing to risk his temper again, I do what he says, and Link crouches down so that he's at my side. He runs his fingertip up and down the length of my ring finger, riding the knuckles before he taps the one closest to the hand, then stands up again.

"Here," he tells Cross. "I want it right here."

"You got it, boss."

Grabbing a tube from his case, he puts a dollop of cream on his finger, then starts applying it to my finger before I can snatch my hand back.

"What's that?" I ask. "It tingles."

"That's good. Means it's working." Cross tosses the tube back into the case, then tugs off his glove. As he pulls on a fresh pair, he explains, "It's a numbing cream. I use it for clients who aren't used to getting ink. I put it on and, twenty minutes later, you won't feel a thing when I get to work." His eyes flicker toward Link. "He insisted."

"I want her to have a permanent ring, Cross, not be in pain."

How kind of him, I think ruefully, glancing down at my bare finger, knowing it won't be like that much longer. I never thought I'd get a tattoo, and it seems almost unreal that I am—and that it's my punishment for the oversized ring slipping off my finger.

Link might not see it that way, but I do. He thinks I did it on purpose, and his solution is to *brand* me like

I'm a fucking animal, all because he thinks making me his wife means that I'm his property.

Too bad there's not a damn thing I can do about it unless I'd rather turn myself in to the police—or see if Damien Libellula still is looking for me.

While we wait for the cream to take effect, Link paces around the room, giving me some space while also obviously unwilling to leave me and Cross alone. I doubt it's a jealous thing; more likely, he's convinced I'll be able to talk my way out of getting this tattoo. Cross has his head bowed over a notepad, doodling ideas for the design that he only shows to Link to get his approval, and I just sit there, waiting for my finger to go numb.

Eventually it does, and Cross picks up his tattoo gun.

He's talented, I'll give him that. He draws his design free-hand, pausing only to wipe away the excess ink with his paper towel squares, and apart from the vague sensation that something is repeatedly tapping my skin, I don't feel a thing as he inks *Lincoln* around my ring finger in a gothic-style swirl.

From a distance, it'll look like I have a black ring inked into my skin, impossible to remove. Up close, though? It says I'm Lincoln's, which surprises me. I would have thought he'd mark me as *Devil*'s—but that's okay.

I insist on that myself.

"Don't put your machine away yet," I tell Cross. It's

the first time I've spoken up since I asked about the numbing cream. "I need another tattoo."

Link firms his jaw. "No, you don't."

Oh, yes. I do.

"What the devil marks as his own... that's what you said to me. I didn't think you meant it literally, but after tonight... I know better now." I jut my chin out. "I'm your pet, Devil. Right? Have him mark me."

"If this is about what happened at the Playground—"

It has *everything* to do with that, but at the same time, if I want to play Link's game, I have to figure out the rules first.

"He grabbed me because I didn't have your mark. I'm your wife. I can't be any more yours, so why shouldn't I have your symbol on my skin? That way everyone knows I'm Lincoln's *and* Devil's."

I thought he would argue more. I thought he would shut my idea down, reminding me that he was in charge.

He doesn't.

Instead, he nods at Cross. "Do it."

Putting down his machine, Cross reaches for the numbing cream.

No.

"I don't want the goop this time," I tell him.

"You'll feel it then."

I meet Link's dark eyes. "I want to feel it."

Cross glances over at my *husband*, looking for his answer.

After a moment, Link nods. "If that's what my wife wants, do it."

As the needle touches my skin, I grit my teeth. The numbing cream fooled me before because, holy shit, it hurts a lot more without it. I refuse to show any sign that it does, though, until he digs a little too deep and I close my eyes, hiding the way tears have filled them.

When I finally open them again, I have a brand new design branded on my forearm—Devil's red horns and the pointed tail curved beneath it—and a missing husband.

Because sometime during my second tattoo, Link left me alone with his men in the penthouse.

the life

Mrs. Crewes

FIFTEEN
SKITTERY

LINCOLN

I probably shouldn't have gone back to the Playground, but I just... *fuck*. I couldn't stay home and watch it as Cross tattooed Ava with my mark like she was a regular member of the syndicate.

I told her I owned her. I needed her to believe it so that she never thought that she could easily push me aside and walk away. After all, I did it to her—and if she really wanted to go, I'd let her; I'd watch her from the shadows like I have, but I'd let her go. No one deserves to be tied to me for life, but if I could convince her that she had to be... I thought I might get to keep her.

But I forgot what a little spitfire my Ava can be. I branded her ring finger with my name, and she retaliated by demanding that Cross mark her with my symbol.

And I couldn't bring myself to bear witness to it.

I tell myself that I'm only going back to the club to make sure that everything has smoothed over after what happened earlier tonight. It isn't often I blow my top with witnesses, and while it's easy to twist the facts so that no one really knows what they saw, someone had to do it.

That was my second, and I beeline right for our usual booth when I see him sitting by himself, a whiskey neat perched in front of him, and his head tossed back.

I slide into the booth. "Everything good, Royce?"

His eyes were closed, snapping open the second my ass hits the seat. His instincts are unmatched, and I know there's no better man to have at my back, even if he shakes his head and says, "Thanks for that, boss. Just what I needed tonight."

I shrug. "He touched my wife."

"Right. Because... and let me stress this part... your unmarked wife was walking in the club without a chaperone, and all the wallets thought she didn't have your protection. Because... again... let me stress this... you'd rather hole her up in your penthouse instead of introducing her to the syndicate so the guys know to protect her, too."

I fucking hate it when he's right. "You don't have to worry about that."

His eyebrows shoot up. "You're finally going to share Saint Ava with the rest of the class."

"Fuck you," I say, but there isn't any heat. "I just meant that she's being marked right now." His eyebrows nearly reach his hairline as I explain, "She asked Cross to do it."

"Riiiight," Royce drawls. "And she happens to know that Cross does all the tats for the Sinners because—"

Ass. "Because I brought him up to the penthouse to ink a ring around her finger because she lost it, okay?"

Slipping his hand into his pants pocket, Royce pulls something out. With a *clink*, the golden band hits the tabletop.

"Where did you find that?"

"A good samaritan found it on the dance floor. They turned it in to the bar. Jessie gave it to me." He uses his finger to shoot it across the table at me. "I guess you won't be needing that now."

I take it anyway. "Thanks."

He shakes his hand, rapping his knuckles against the tabletop. "I don't get it, Link. I just don't fucking get it."

"There's nothing to get, Royce."

You think he'd know me well enough to take a hint. Not my second.

"Look at you. You're puppy dog awful over this woman... have been as long as I've known you... and you're hiding her. If it was me, I'd be showing her off to everyone in Springfield. But you... I still don't get why you let her get away in the first place."

He doesn't, does he? "I had to. It was my penance."

Royce snorts. "Catholic shit, huh?"

Something like that.

"I wasn't good for her." I'm still not. "Right before I left... I killed a guy."

He points a finger at me. "You've killed plenty."

True. "Yeah, but he was my first."

"Ah. Just like with women, you always remember your first kill."

He doesn't know how right he is. "I was a runner, Royce. A fighter. But a killer? Shit, I was *twenty*. A *kid*. What did I know about killin' anyone? But when my old boss told me to work him over because he owed him money, that I'd get a cut of it... he shouldn't have said what he said. I wouldn't have done what I did if he didn't threaten her."

Royce knows this part of the story.

Everyone in the life knows this part.

His name was Skittery. A nickname, of course, and he got it from how antsy and jittery and, well, skittery he got when he was coming down from whatever junk he was on. He had a smart mouth, sticky fingers, but I heard he had a habit of sticking his dick into women who weren't willing.

There's a reason the Sinners went into girls. We make sure that everyone who has a spot upstairs wants it. No one is forced to sell themselves for money, and for a percent of the profits, we make sure of it.

But the Sinners didn't exist back then. Neither did the Libellula Family. Instead, there were six, seven, eight small gangs in Springfield, each fighting over a scrap of territory.

I worked under a guy named Gunner. Fitting, since he's the one who got me into gun-running for money in the first place, but I was still making a living with street fights at that point.

Until Skittery owed Gunner money, and I was tasked with getting it back. No force was too unnecessary, and Gunnar said I could kill him if he didn't have the dough. He was that done with Skittery.

I never thought I had it in me. Sure, there was always that darkness welling up inside of me—a shadow that was only tamed by Ava's sunshine—but a murderer? It went against the commandments. I couldn't do it.

And then Skittery made the last mistake of his life. He spat at me when I asked for Gunner's money, and he laughed at me. I could deal with that... until he said with a cocky grin that he was going to find Ava and fuck her brainless to get back at me for trying to buck up to him.

He didn't call her my girl. He used her name.

He mentioned that she was in college.

He *knew* who she was—and he threatened to touch her.

No one touches Ava like that. I knew that even then and I... I didn't just kill him. With the only weapon I had—my fists—I beat that junkie to death. Then, when I was done, I took the knife I found on him and hacked his head right off of his body.

You wouldn't think that's possible. Trust me. With enough icy rage, determination, and blacking out after the first couple of hits, I cut and I stabbed and I hacked until I severed that fucker's head from his neck.

The whole thing happened in an alley in the rundown part of Springfield where I lived with Ava. There were enough people passing by as witness that I couldn't even deny what I'd done if I wanted to. One local in particular stumbled upon me when I had just finished hacking through the spinal cord, seeing me hoist up Skittery's detached head, telling it in a cold voice that I'll see him in hell, and... yeah. That was that.

The legend of the Devil of Springfield was born that day—and Lincoln Crewes died, himself. Staring at the blood on my hands, I knew that I could never touch Ava again not what I knew I was capable of such brutality. Taking nothing more than my rosary and my phone, I walked away from her that day, knowing that there was a chance I'd never see my beloved Ava again.

To be honest, I expected to leave downtown Springfield and walk right into a cell—or a bullet. Nope. Gunner shielded me from the crooked cops the same way I protected Ava after she shot Maglione, but he owned me from then on; even if I didn't leave Ava, I would've had to once I fell further into the life. I was my old boss's until the day one of his rivals took him out, and after everything I did for Gunner—the crimes I committed, the people I killed—I knew I couldn't go back to Ava just yet.

Instead, I started my own syndicate.

It was my penance. I spent fifteen years trying to make up for putting her in danger that one time, using my new reputation and power to protect her from the shadows. I always vowed to myself that, when I did, when I had enough power, enough wealth, and enough control over my dark side to risk returning to her, I finally would. Until then, I would do whatever I could to watch over her, keeping her safe from a distance.

And then I fucked up by letting a Dragonfly slip past me, Joey Maglione tried to do what Skittery had threatened long ago, and here I am.

God, I need a fucking drink.

Before I can flag down a waitress, I notice that Royce is watching me with an amused smile.

"What?" I snap.

The cocky grin widens. "I finally figured it out."

"Figured what out?"

"Why you went so long without getting laid. It's because your game with women fucking sucks."

Even now, the idea of touching anyone besides Ava has my hands curling into fists.

"I haven't gotten laid in fifteen years because the only woman I've ever wanted is Ava," I remind him.

Royce laughs, rising up from his seat, leaning across the booth to clap me on the shoulder. "You're just proving my point. After all that time, you finally have her back, and what are you doing? Dicking around with me at the Playground while she's back at your penthouse? You should get home, boss. Trust me. I got things handled here."

"Royce—"

His lips twitch, forcing another smile. "Hey. I've got a reason to be in this hellhole all the damn time. You don't."

I shut my fucking mouth. Because you know what?

We both know he's right about that—and, all right. The other stuff, too.

"Thanks, buddy. You're right. I'm going home."

And when I get there, I'm starting over with Ava.

I vow it.

the life

Mrs. Crewes

SIXTEEN
WHORE

AVA

The night that I visited the Devil's Playground for the first time, I thought my marriage was over. Seeing how determined Link was to claim me as his—beating that guy up, throwing him out of the club, then coming back to the penthouse with Cross so that he could tattoo a wedding band on my finger—made me understand the lengths he'll go to maintain the facade that we're really in it 'til death do us part.

I'll admit, though, that as another few weeks pass, it's getting harder and harder to tell myself that it's a facade.

He's trying. Because he is, I am, too.

There's only one big point of contention that we have: my babysitters.

I would've thought that, after I got Bobby in trouble for how I snuck past him, Link might've realized how ridiculous it was to insist that I have one or two strangers watching over me whenever he was busy. Nope. It was the opposite, actually. He tried to arrange a rotation like I was one of my students, for God's sake. Only when I threatened to return to my house—leaving the penthouse entirely—did he back off down.

I still have babysitters. They're just not on a schedule, so it's easy to pretend that the random armed men moving around the penthouse are like maintenance men or something.

I've learned to ignore them. I had to. They're not my friends. At most, they're Link's employees, and I never forget for a minute that their loyalty is to him.

Mona, too. She's sweet to me, and if it wasn't for her, I'd go stir crazy when Link was busy out of the penthouse, but it's obvious that she's keeping tabs on me, reporting back to Mr. Lincoln whenever she gets the chance.

At least, when it comes to my actions, she does, and I know it's because Link makes her. Same with the guards.

But while they're happy to report on me to my husband, they definitely keep their feelings about me to themselves—because, one thing for sure, if Link heard what I did one afternoon, I'm pretty sure he would've lost his shit.

I mean, he beat a guy to a bloody pup for touching

me. I highly doubt he'd stand by and let his own men question our marriage.

Only they are, and I find out completely by accident.

I'm in the kitchen with Mona, "helping" her make lunch. Cooking has never been my strong suit, so I'm probably being a nuisance more than anything, but Link left early this morning and I like to feel like I'm doing something.

And, honestly, there's only so much TV a woman can watch before she wants to chuck the remote at the screen—and, considering Link's television is like seventy freaking inches across, I wouldn't miss.

Leaning against the counter, watching as Mona stirs the stew for today's lunch, I hear a pair of footsteps coming down the hall. Heavy boots hit the floor, just out of step with each other, and I realize that since there are two of them out there, it's probably the changing of the guards.

I've watched it happen as I sat on the couch in the living room, either watching TV or reading a book I nabbed from the library. The men always seem to talk in code—something Link has a tendency to do, too, as if I'm too delicate to hear about all the awful things the Devil does—but I get the gist they're talking about me.

They are now, only this time? It's not in code.

They probably think they don't have to since I'm not in the living room to overhear them.

Oh, no. I'm in the kitchen with Mona, and I can hear every word.

"Hey, Twig." It sounds like the guard who's been here all morning. "You up next?"

"Oh, yeah," comes a second, more nasal voice. "I pissed off my handler and he decided it was my turn to spend an evening with the boss's bitch. What about you? How'd you get stuck with the job?"

"Me? Oh. I offered."

"Yeah?"

The first man chuckles. "Yeah. She's easy on the eyes and stays to herself. Quiet, too. I don't mind watching her for the boss."

"Hey. You never know. With a girl like that, you might have a chance when he's done with her. I've heard that he's never been seen with a chick before. Like some of the fellas started thinking he was a fag, right? Not anymore. He proved us wrong."

I can't believe I'm hearing this. Link told me that there hasn't been anyone but me since we broke up—and I still have a hard time believing *that*—and that he was too busy to find a wife, but that it was expected of him. Is this why? Because rumors run that he's gay?

He's not. Not completely, at any rate. For all I know, he could've been with a hundred guys and still mean it when he says that I was the only woman he's been with. There's no faking his attraction to me. That's one thing that's never been in doubt. That man lives to fuck me, but why are these two talking about me like I might be up for grabs eventually?

Mona is still stirring the stew, back to the threshold. I can't tell if she's oblivious to the conversation—or if she's pretending not to hear it.

I should do the same... but I don't.

I *can't*.

"I guess," continues the first guy. "He seems attached to this one, but if he changes his mind... I like 'em sweet."

"A sweet whore," Twig sneers. "Ain't that an oxymoron or some shit."

"Twig..."

"What? To be honest, I still can't believe Devil finally took one of the whores home with him. I mean, shit. It's one thing to pick one out and fuck 'em upstairs. But the move 'em into his place and act like she's better than the rest... she must be a fucking amazing lay, that's all I'm gonna say."

Oh my God. They're still talking about me, aren't they?

Mona stops stirring the stew.

"You know something," says the first guy. "I heard he *married* her."

"Bullshit." That's Twig again. "Sinners fuck whores, they don't marry 'em."

I look at my ring finger. It took days of wearing the ointment Cross left with Link before the swelling went down and the tattoo healed enough that the script—*Lincoln*—was legible.

He married me. In the dead of night, with only a judge to witness it, he married me... and two of his employees are debating it as if they have no idea that it's true.

But he told me. He told me that he needed a wife to run the syndicate. He needed a wife and... and an *heir*.

He *told* me.

He didn't tell the Sinners.

I wrap my arms around my middle, wishing that the floor would just open up and swallow me whole. I'd put fifty bucks down that these two think I'm in a totally different part of the penthouse and that they had no idea I heard everything they just said. I can't bring myself to leave the kitchen in case I run into them and have to see their distaste for me on their face.

I can't.

Mona can.

Whether she missed out on the first part of their conversation or it hit a point where she just couldn't ignore it any longer, the grandmotherly housekeeper finally snaps.

Laying her wooden spoon on the spoon rest, she wipes her hands on her apron, storming across the kitchen. When she reaches the threshold, she perches her hand on her hips.

"You talk like that in Ms. Ava's home, tak? When she can hear you?"

Oh, God. This is even more embarrassing. I mean, I know what Mama Mona is doing. Like always, she's standing up for her children, but I was hoping I can slink out of here without passing the two gangsters.

Welp. Not now.

Because staying hidden in the kitchen would make me look like a coward in addition to being a *whore,* I join her at the threshold, looking at the two men who were talking about me.

One is the shaggy-haired, twenty-something who's been here all afternoon. The other is a skinny blonde with a perpetual smirk and an ill-fitting suit. I don't recognize him—he must be a new soldier on babysitting duty—but his dark eyes look right through me.

Next to me, Mona says something in Polish, too fast for me to pick up any of the words I've learned from her. Whatever it is, she's obviously scolding them, and the one with the shaggy hair actually looks contrite; he must understand the language. The other one just throws a leer at me.

Right. Because I'm Devil's whore, huh?

And despite how often he calls me his wife, or the fact that he branded me with his name, I can't even argue that they're wrong.

It'll be real from the moment you say 'I do'

For me, maybe. Obviously not for Link.

Pushing past the leering asshole, leaving Mona to

ream them out again, I disappear down the hall. I can't find it in me to go to our bedroom right now, and I let myself into Link's library, flopping down on the chaise lounge I've never seen him use.

Right. Because he's rarely fucking *here*.

Oh, Ava... I always knew I was naive.

I guess I thought, by the time I reached my mid-thirties, I'd have grown out of it.

Too bad I obviously haven't.

the life

Mrs. Crewes

SEVENTEEN
DINNERTIME

LINCOLN

Having dinner with Ava is the highlight of my day.

There's something about coming home to a shy smile and a homemade meal, sitting down at the table with her, and just talking about regular shit. I don't have to talk about the hits I approved or ordered, the guns that arrived at the warehouse, or how much the Playground made overnight.

We have an unspoken rule that, when we're together at home, I can go back to being Lincoln—to being Ava's *Link*—while leaving Devil and all that poor bastard's responsibilities and dark reputation at the door.

Do I know that I'm fooling myself?

Of course I do. I can't *not* be Devil any more than I

can go back in time and return to being the boy that Ava first fell in love with. But can I do whatever it takes to make my wife fall in love with me again?

Fuck if I know, but I'm going to try.

I bring her flowers. I ask her about her day, and she lies about how much she doesn't hate being trapped in the penthouse. I promise to take her out before, inevitably, my business phone rings and I have to grab another soldier to watch over her while I go out to take care of things...

Maybe it's not what I thought married life would be like when I fantasized about marrying Ava Monroe when I was seventeen, but we're still working things out. It's only been a month, and while I'm damn sure to spend every night in bed with my wife, everything's still new for both of us. I still lose my temper when I think about that stupid bastard who laid his hands on my Ava. Add that to how Burns keeps me updated on how the "search" for "missing person" Joseph Maglione is going—strong-armed by a member of the Libellula Family, the cop confirms—and I can't risk letting her step foot out of the penthouse again unless I'm right there at her side.

When we're sitting in the dining room, sharing a meal, chatting about stupid shit like a real couple, I can fool myself into thinking that she *chose* me. That she wanted me as her husband instead of being forced into saying 'I do' with me.

I'm getting pretty good at it, and then reality comes

crashing down on an ordinary Tuesday night while we're eating the steak and mashed potatoes that Mona served for dinner.

I'm almost done with my meal when I notice that Ava has spent more time moving the food around her plate than eating it.

"What's wrong, pet? You've been quiet all night."

As though she's trying desperately to find some normalcy in our "relationship", Ava acts like the girl I remember whenever we're alone. She's chatty and smart, witty and thoughtful, silly and sweet. She's mine, and I spend every minute away from her counting down the seconds until I can tuck a stray strand behind her ear as she tells me another story about her last group of first-graders.

I'm head over heels for a teacher. Part of me is so fucking proud that she lived out her dreams, that she didn't let me going off the rails the way that I did throw her off *her* path. The other side—the darker side that's *Devil*—wonders how she's going to react when I eventually tell her that she won't be going back to Springfield Elementary in September.

I couldn't risk it. Set aside how a school is a dangerous place these days because of fuckers with no brains and guns that I never would've passed into their hands. Sooner or later, all of Springfield is going to know that she's the Devil's bride. It won't be safe for her out there.

I don't know if it's safe for her in here, either, but that's where she's going to stay.

Tonight, something's on her mind. I wonder if it's because she's figured that out, but then she looks up from her barely-touched food and says, "Did you mean it?"

"Mean what?"

"When you said that this was a real marriage... did you mean it?"

I drop my fork to my plate. "Why are you asking me that?"

I thought we got this shit out of the way. From the moment I claimed her in the judge's bathroom, she was mine, and there was no going back. For God's sake, she has my name wrapped around her finger—just like she has *me* wrapped around her finger—and she still doubts that I'm dead-fucking-serious about spending the rest of my life with her?

What else do I have to do to prove that she's mine?

"It's nothing," she says, pushing her potatoes around the plate.

The fuck it is. "Ava. Tell me."

She exhales.

I grip the table, so tight my knuckles turn white.

Pretty green eyes flicker my way. "No."

I'm glad she feels comfortable enough to deny the monster in her midst. I don't ever want Ava to fear me the same way the rest of Springfield does, and I thought I lost the sliver of affection I garnered from her after I showed my true colors at the Playground.

But this is different. The whole conversation started because she can't shake the idea that our marriage is fake.

I'll get her to see that it couldn't be any more real if it's the death of me—or someone else.

"If you don't tell me, I'll get them to." And they won't like my ways of getting them to talk. "Mona, too. If they're talking shit in front of my wife, I know she heard them."

"No," yelps Ava. "She stood up for me."

Ah. "Mona," I call, lifting my voice so that my housekeeper can hear me. "Come here, please."

"Link... it's fine. I shouldn't have said anything."

Yes. She should.

"You will always tell me when something is bothering you," I say firmly, waiting for Mona to bustle her way into the living room. "I want to know, especially if it's something that I can fix."

"You've done enough for me—"

"I'm your husband," I remind her, hating how cold I sound as I say that. It's better than raging—which part of me wants to do—but not by much. "I will do *everything* I can for you."

"Link..."

I've said what I had to about that. Turning as Mona appears in the doorway, I hold up my hand. She comes to a stop, a curious look on her weathered features.

"You called for me, Mr. Lincoln?"

"Yes. I was just talking to my wife and she mentioned that there might have been a few of my men not treating her with the respect she deserves. Now, we both know how sweet Ava is." As Mona nods in agreement, I try to keep the predator's edge out of my grin as I add, "And we know what kind of man I am. So, please, as a favor to me... what did they say?"

I've known Mama Mona since I was four. She's always treated me as her own, and when I found out she was being evicted from her shitty apartment through a landlord's slimy loophole all because it was rent-controlled, I moved her in with me, giving her a job, and a second lease on life.

My mother kicked me out on my eighteenth birthday. I'd stopped thinking of her as any kind of maternal figure long before she did. That was all Mona.

Sometimes I think she still has some idyllic idea of who Lincoln Crewes is. Deep down, she has to know how I built my wealth, but she's spent eight years pretending that she doesn't.

As she wrings her hand together, looking from me to Ava and back, I'm sure she's weighing how much to tell me.

That right there is a big clue that I'm not going to like it.

"Mona. Please."

Her bottom lip trembles. "Oh, Mr. Lincoln. They think she's... I can't say it. It was so cruel."

Cruel? "I still want to know."

"Whore," snaps my wife. "Happy? I heard one of them joke that you finally fell for one of the whores, okay? And they were looking right at me when I heard them talking about it." She lets her own fork fall to her plate, covering her face with her hand. "It was humiliating."

"I'm so sorry, Mr. Lincoln. I sent them away, and I was going to tell you—"

"But I told her not to," Ava cuts in, speaking through the gaps in her fingers. "It's not her fault they got the wrong idea about me." She pauses, dropping her eyes to the table. "About us."

No. It's not Mona's fault, is it?

It's *mine*.

Ice floods my veins. I haven't felt that sort of detachment since the fateful night when I hacked Skittery's head off of his neck, but it hits me now as I realize just how oblivious I was in my happiness.

So damn pleased that I maneuvered Ava into being my wife, I was blind to how some of the men were treating her. Just because they got their kicks, getting close to the girls at the club, somehow they got the idea that Ava was one of them.

It's my fucking fault. I didn't make it clear enough after the altercation at the club. Those in my inner circle—my underboss, my counselors—they know she's my wife. The soldiers just know she's to be protected.

Lord knows rumors spread, too. I beat the shit out of a wallet for trying to bring Ava upstairs, so why wouldn't some of the lower-ranked syndicate members get the idea that she was another one of the sex workers at the Playground.

But for her to hear them… for her to think that's what she is to me… for my Ava to even doubt for one second that she's the most important person in this world to me?

That she's my goddamn *wife*?

It's my fucking fault—but I'll fix it. I'll find out from Mona who exactly spoke about my wife like that in her hearing, and I'll take care of them.

And that's not all.

What do I have to prove that she's mine?

Show those who are putting doubts in my Ava's pretty little head that I'm *hers*.

the life

Mrs. Crewes

EIGHTEEN
ON DISPLAY

LINCOLN

The Devil's Playground isn't just our moneymaker.

It's our headquarters.

It only made sense. The more powerful the Sinners Syndicate became, the more space we needed. What started as a small bar turned into a half-a-block-wide structure as we bought more and more property, building onto it. The second floor became the spot dedicated to the working girls, the back rooms were where the gamblers went to spend their dough, and the office space next door was where the Sinners met.

It's not always about business. There's a gaming area inside, complete with a billiards table, dartboards, and three vintage arcade games. We have a separate bar for the syndicate, an on-site cook, and a swimming pool.

But, on the rare occasion that I call a syndicate meet instead of one-on-ones, we have a conference room that rivals anything in corporate America.

The conference room has a long ass table, at least twenty seats, the most boring carpet in the world, and no windows. I hate the fucking place. I only go in there when I need to, when I have to remind the gang that I'm in charge, or when I'm meeting with the mayor of Springfield and his cronies. Dumb prick insists on "privacy", as though I don't have eyes on him and his twinks at all times, or know that he spends as much time schmoozing with Damien as he does me and my men.

Today, I have my men all lined up at the wall. The seats are stacked together, shoved to the far side of the room, leaving only the empty table in the middle.

Well, it's empty for now, but it won't be much longer...

Ava is standing next to me. Under the scrutiny of the Sinners, she tried to duck behind me, but I want to show off my gorgeous bride. She has her light brown hair styled in soft curls today, her green eyes bright, her creamy skin so damn touchable... and I can't wait until I can. Taking her hand, I tug her into my side, letting her know she has my protection while also keeping her front and center in front of the men.

I make a noise in the back of my throat. Each one stops glancing at Ava, focusing on me entirely.

Good.

"Evening, fellas. I'm gonna make this quick because I'm wasting precious time with my new bride"—the first murmurs erupt before Royce waves a hand gesturing for them to shut the hell up—"and I'd rather be with her than looking at your ugly mugs. But I figured it was time to introduce you to her, so I gathered you here for a quick announcement and a demonstration. First, the announcement." I still have Ava's hand clasped in mine. Lifting it high, making sure they can see the dark lines of my name on her all-important ring finger, I say, "This is Ava Crewes. For those who don't know, she is my wife. We eloped last month, and now that I've had her to myself for a while, I thought it was time to introduce her to the syndicate."

The men who have met her previously all nod their acknowledgment. Ava squeezes my fingers, obviously aware of the confusion, interest, and distrust coming from those who are just now hearing about her.

That's okay. I set up this meet to prove to her—the syndicate, too, but mostly her—that she's mine, and I'm ready to do that.

No matter what it takes.

"Now, I'm not a fucking idiot. I know there's been talk of me stepping down because I didn't want a wife before. For some reason, the Sinners think I'm dying to get an heir, but if that's what you guys want from your leader, fine. I got a wife, but even then some of you are doubters." I run my gaze over all of them. "Sham marriage. Fake marriage... for fuck's sake, it's gotten back to me that some of you fuckers think she's my beard. Well, I'm more than happy to show you just how much your boss loves pussy."

Ava turns to me, eyes wide in shock. I expected that. When I told her I wanted to present her to the Sinners, I instructed her to wear a short dress I bought just for the occasion—and not to bother with panties. She's gotten better at giving up putting that scrap of a barrier between us, and I checked her myself earlier when Luca was driving us over to the Playground.

She's ready for me, and I'm ready for this.

Leaning in, brushing my stubbled jaw against her cheek, I whisper, "You're gonna love this."

"Link, I don't think—"

"Do you trust your husband?"

"Well, yeah, but—"

"Then trust me. Keep your eyes on me and just enjoy the ride."

I pull back before Ava can say another word. Letting go of her hand, I grip her waist, lifting her easily. We'd been standing to the side of the conference table so all it takes is a twist and a turn before she's propped up on the edge of it.

One shove. That's all it takes to get the hem of her dress out of my way.

Then, dropping to my knees, I ignore the murmurs

and comments from the men as I lay my hands on her thighs.

"It's just me and you, Ava," I tell her, putting a small amount of pressure on her to spread her legs wide. "Don't look at them. Keep your eyes on me and open up for your husband."

I don't force her—I never would—but I show her what I want.

After a moment's hesitation, she gives it to me, baring her damp pussy to me. Her curls are already glistening with her need.

That's my girl.

Turned on more by the fact that we have an audience than how she has the most powerful fucker in all of the city at her mercy, she's already keening before I get my hot mouth on her cunt.

Once I do, Ava closes her eyes, throwing back her head, writhing as if she can't get enough of me.

Perfect. She's reacting just like I thought she would, and she's motherfucking *perfect*.

Leaning back, I reach up, snagging one of her hands. "Pull my hair," I murmur, loud enough for the others to hear. "Grab on tight. I'm only just getting started, pet."

I know what the guys have to be thinking. No one touches Devil. Idiots have earned broken fingers for just brushing up against me, and here I am, feasting on Ava's pussy while encouraging her to thread her fingers through my hair.

That alone should've been enough to prove my point. Just in case it isn't, I massage her thighs, ripping pants, grunts, and moan out of my wife as I nuzzle her clit, flicking it with my tongue before returning my attention to lapping at her entrance.

As soon as I feel like I've made my point, I stop drawing it out. Dedicating everything I have in me to making my wife come, I slip two of my fingers inside of her, giving her something to clench as I nibble her clit, then suck her labia into my mouth as I fingerfuck her to completion.

When I have, I don't wipe my mouth. With my lips shiny from Ava's juices, I pat her thighs closed, go to one knee, then the other, and rise up to my full height so they can all see how much I enjoyed letting Ava ride my face in front of them.

Eyes blazing at every Sinner assembled in the conference room, I tell them, "This woman is Ava Crewes. She's my wife. My *everything*. And I want each of you to know that she owns *me*. Got that?"

For a moment, there's absolute silence, but then Royce whistles between his teeth. Following his lead, applause breaks out, all of the men calling out their congratulations to Ava and me.

Over the roar of their congratulations, one of the men scoffs.

Like a shark zeroing in on its prey, I get the blond in my sights. Silence falls as I take a few pointed steps toward him.

"Twig." The single syllable is like ice. "You got something to say?"

"Well, yeah, boss. I get that she's your wife and all now, but that doesn't change the way things work around here."

Is that so?

"Oh? And how do things work?"

Royce shakes his head. Killian, standing on the other side of Twig, takes a noticeable step away from him.

Smart.

Twig doesn't notice. "You know. She's yours. I get that we gotta munch some pussy to keep our ladies happy, but you're the boss. If you wanted to prove that she belongs to you, she should've been sucking your dick instead."

Why would she when the whole purpose of his public display was so that there wasn't a single doubt let in her mind—and the syndicate's—about her place in my life?

"Didn't you hear me? This woman owns *me*."

"I don't know, boss. I still think she should've been the one to go to her knees."

My fingers flex. "What? Like a whore?"

For the first time, he looks a little uneasy. "I didn't say that."

Yes. He did.

"Link," murmurs Ava. "I want to go home."

Not yet. "She should've gone to her knees, right?

You said that." When Twig opens his mouth, I cut him off before he can say another word. "Don't deny it. Come on, Twiggy. We're all Sinners here. What if I said I'd let her go to her knees for you. You think you can handle my wife?"

Ava reaches out, touching the back of my arm. "Lincoln."

There's no Lincoln here. No Link, either.

Only the Devil.

Now, I don't know what the fuck this kid thinks being a Sinner means, because sharing girls... that shit doesn't fly here. After that happened to Royce... even if my guys wanted to share, I put a stop to that years ago. Twig hasn't been a soldier long enough to figure that out, I guess.

Too bad.

Shaking Ava off of me, I gesture at Twig. "Go on. Take it out, big guy. Show us what you got."

"Don't do it," Royce mutters out of the corner of his mouth. "Just drop it and hope Devil does, too."

Twig is a stupid son of a bitch. My second gave him a chance to back down. Doing his job, coming between me and the rest of the Sinners, Royce was trying to save Twig's dumb ass.

It doesn't work.

Twig jerks his chin at me. "Yeah, boss. Alright. And because she's your woman, I'll try my best not to gag her."

Ava gasps, and I drop my hand, waggling my

fingers, sending her a wordless message not to let what this idiot is saying get to her.

I'm straight as an arrow, but I'd rather suck a cock myself than ever watch Ava go down on another guy.

Twig doesn't know that, though—but he will.

I look forward to it, too.

Now, if he'd been limp, expecting Ava's mouth to get him hard, I might've given him a pass for his little stunt. I'd still teach him a lesson—especially since Mona identified him as one of the mouths talking shit about my wife—but things might have been different. Going down on Ava, showing the rest of the syndicate just how much power she has over me... that wasn't meant to get them off. It was meant to show them that she was my queen.

But Twig doesn't have a flaccid cock, or even one that's semi-hard. Oh, no. It's a full-blown erection, and he yanks it out of his pants with a smirk on his face that tells me he's already imagining what it'll be like to have Ava's lush lips wrapped around him.

He pulls out his cock.

I pull out my piece.

Over the sudden silence, I hear Ava suck in a breath—and Royce mutter, "Fucking moron," under his.

He knows. My second knows what's coming.

I don't disappoint.

With a steady hand and no emotion on my face, I

aim for his exposed dick. One shot and, instead of my wife blowing him, Devil blows it the fuck off.

Close enough, right?

Twig barely gets the chance to rip a high-pitch squeal before I shift my hold on the gun, lifting it just high enough before putting a single bullet through his skull.

He's dead before he hits the industrial carpet.

Royce stepped aside so that he was out of the spatter zone. Killian curses when he sees that he ended up with Twig's blood on his suit because he was too slow to get out of the way, but he shuts his trap when I turn my gaze on him.

"Does anyone else think it's a good idea to disrespect my wife?"

Behind me, Ava is panting softly. She's probably close to hyperventilating, and I'm sorry she had to see Devil take control, but that dumb fuck thought I would let her suck his cock. My *Ava* on her knees for another man...

She goes to her knees for God—and for Devil. No one else.

And I want every Sinner to know it. If I have to exterminate my whole crew for her, I would.

I'd burn the fucking world down for this woman if I had to, and I'd offer her the match to blow out when I was done.

When no one else proves to have a death wish like Twig did, I nod at them.

"Leave us."

There isn't any hesitation. Knowing I'm dead fucking serious—and that my Sig Sauer has more than enough rounds to take out anyone else who looks at me twice—the Sinners scatter.

The only one who lingers is Royce. Grabbing two guys by their jackets—Frankie and Julio—he jerks his chin down at Twig's body.

After a quick game of rock-papers-scissors that Frankie wins, he grabs Twig's boots. Julio wrinkles his nose and wordlessly picks the dead man up by his arms. They carry him out of the conference room.

Royce salutes me, then follows after them, closing the door behind him.

I've regained some of my composure. Thawing out a little now that I know Twig got what he deserved, I turn slowly so that I can face Ava.

She's a little shocky—like I expected—though her voice is steadier than I thought it would be as she says, "You killed him."

I did. "He disrespected you."

"But... you *killed* him."

The idea seems so foreign to her, I almost feel sorry to have to rip the wool away from her eyes.

"It's not the first time I've pulled the trigger," I shrug. Especially for Ava's sake. "It won't be the last, either."

"But don't you feel bad? You killed him like it was—"

"Easy?" I supply.

She nods. "Yes."

"It is." Now. "And, no, I don't feel bad at all."

I see understanding dawn in her eyes, followed by something I pretend isn't horror. "You really are the Devil, aren't you?"

I stay quiet because what can I say? She's not wrong.

Ava takes a few steps back before moving around me. "You don't have any feelings at all, at least not about me. You don't care that you embarrassed the hell out of me, putting me on display like that—"

"I only did it because I knew you would get off harder than you ever had with all those eyes on you."

Ava scoffs, but she doesn't deny it. She can't. When it comes to her exhibitionist tendencies, we both know I'm right about that.

Instead, she snaps, "So? You still killed a guy because of your precious rep," before turning her back on me.

I let her take a few steps, then admit that I was full of shit before when I said I'd let her go. Hell, no. This woman is *never* getting away from me.

"I have feelings," I toss after her before she can cross the room.

She goes still.

"I have feelings, Ava," I repeat. "Lust. Anger. *Obsession*. God, when I think of you, I want you so bad, that I'll do anything for you. And you got it wrong. Killing

Twig... I could give a shit about my rep. I did it so my men know that they're not untouchable. When it comes to you, my Ava... I'd kill every last one of them for you."

The weight of that realization has her swallowing roughly. It's probably way too much for her, but she gets past it quickly, instead focusing on something else entirely.

"What happened to calling me 'pet'?" she tosses back at me.

"I still own you. There's no reason to call you my pet when I can call you *mine*."

She seems to like that answer. Moving into me, biting the corner of her mouth as if she has something to say but doesn't know how to say it, she finally spits it out.

"All those feelings you talked about Link... there's one you didn't mention. What about love?"

Is she serious? I love her more than life itself.

This close, I can touch her. Collaring her throat, I tilt her head back, meeting the defiant look on her face —and the undeniable fear in her green gaze.

My stomach flip-flops. I've never seen her look at me like that. It's only for a split second, there and gone again, but I saw it.

And I know I'll only scare her more if I tell her that I never stopped loving her.

"What do you think?" I sneer, taking her mouth, swallowing any answer she might've had.

As she clings to me, tasting herself on my lips, falling into me as though resigned to the fact that this is her life now, I wonder what she would've said.

It doesn't matter.

She finally understands just who she married.

What she married.

I'm the Devil of Springfield, and she's my wife—whether she wants to be or not.

the life

Mrs. Crewes

NINETEEN
COMES FIRST

AVA

Everyone in the Sinners Syndicate treats me like I'm Devil's wife after that—everyone, that is, except for the one man who counts.

I don't know exactly what happened. He was the one who brought me in front of all of his men. He was the one who insisted on hoisting me up on the table before burying his face in my pussy. He ordered me to ride his face, to pull his hair, to come... and then, when I'd barely come down from my orgasm, he killed a smart-mouthed man in front of all of us.

In that moment, I knew that my Link was gone— and that's assuming that any part of the kind, dedicated, devoted boy he'd been was still lingering inside of him. I'd had glimpses of the Devil before—the way he glared at Joey's corpse, and how he beat that man half to death at the club—but when he calmly pulled his gun out and shot one of his soldiers point-blank like that?

I finally understood why everyone in Springfield whispers his name in fear alongside Damien Libellula. He isn't just dangerous. Devil is wicked. He's heartless.

And I'm supposed to be his bride.

Maybe I'm wrong. Running my thumb over the healed ink, covering his name from the *L* to the *n*, then going back again, I wonder if I said 'I do' to Lincoln Crewes, and now that Devil has reared his head, he no longer thinks of me as his wife.

I guess that makes sense. Since the scene in the conference room two weeks ago, there hasn't been a single whisper that our marriage is a sham. Any time one of the Sinners stops by the penthouse, I get a nod instead of a knowing sneer. They murmur, "Mrs. Crewes," in a voice full of respect; no more murmurs that I'm the Devil's whore, or whispers that I'm his beard. Link might not have gone so far as to lay me out on the conference room's table, fucking me for all of his men to see, but eating me out in front of them did the trick.

Not only did it prove that Link wasn't afraid of vagina, but he showed them all just how much he honored me by going to his knees rather than ordering me to go to mine.

I know I shouldn't, but I regret throwing it in his face that his act embarrassed me. For one, I knew what

I was getting into when I agreed to marry him. Though so much of learning about Link's world is an education, I went into this fully aware that he was the head of the Sinners Syndicate. He was a crime boss with at least thirty loyal soldiers under him.

The Springfield mafias do things differently. They let their actions speak much louder than any words. Whether by using their firsts, their weapons, or—in this case—their wicked mouths, they have to show they mean business.

He didn't have any problem performing a sex act on me with all of his men watching. Of the two of us, it was Link I had to coax and tease to get him to go along with the thrill of fucking where we could be caught. Pleasuring me where the Sinners had no choice *but* to watch? That would've bothered the old Link way more than me.

He wasn't wrong when he told me I'd like it. If he'd eased me to my back, hanging my legs off the edge of the table after he made me come the first time, I would've eagerly welcomed him whipping out his dick. At that moment, I would've let him fuck me gladly, and not given a single crap who was watching.

But he didn't. Instead, he encouraged Twig to take out his.

I still remember the fleeting sense of betrayal that had me hopping down from the table, moving into Link. If there was one thing I thought was clear about our arrangement, it was that we were monogamous. He wouldn't take any mistresses, and I wouldn't have to worry about another guy getting with me.

What happened that night in the Playground was supposed to have made that obvious—but then he stood there, entertaining the idea that I would suck off Twig.

I don't know why I even let myself believe that Link would ever do that. In hindsight, the idea that he would kill Twig instead of standing back and watching me pleasure the other man was so much more believable... but until he fired his gun, it never occurred to me that he would.

I know better now.

This is the life, Ava. Welcome to it.

I get that. And if this is who Link is, I accept that. That doesn't change the fact that he's still the boy I once loved—and the man that, despite showing me different facets of the complicated Devil he's become, I thought I was falling for again.

He's a murderer. An *obsessed* murderer, I admit, and for the first few weeks, I was the target of his obsession. From the gifts he bought—ranging from a first edition copy of my favorite book to jewelry, flowers, and a laptop that probably cost more than two months of my mortgage that someone named Tanner tricked out for me—and the way he hung on every word I said when we had dinner together, plus how devoted to wringing as many orgasms out of me as he could when we were in bed... even if he couldn't love me, I knew he at least felt something for me.

He admitted as much after I accused him of not having any feelings at all.

Lust, he said.

Anger.

Obsession.

Not love, but that's okay. I can love him enough for both of us—and when Link spends the next two weeks after his big demonstration growing more and more distant from me, I have to.

It starts out with his missing dinner once or twice. He's busy. Busier than normal, from the snippets of conversation I pick up, listening in on his conversations with whatever Sinner he has watching over me. Even Mona notices it, assuring me that Link is in the middle of something.

Fine.

But when I go an entire night without him, only waking up as he slipped, exhausted and fully dressed, into our bed at six-thirty in the morning, I begin to think his obsession with me is fading.

He doesn't initiate. It's the first time since he took me in Judge Callihan's bathroom that he doesn't at least hold me close; when I was on my period and didn't feel like sex, he snuggled, stealing gentle kisses all night long while holding the heating pad in place to ease my cramps.

I thought he'd be pissed that he didn't knock me

up, but he wasn't. He just smiled and said, "That's just more time I get with only you, my Ava."

My Ava...

I stopped being his 'pet' after he brought me to the Playground to introduce me to the Sinners. I'm his Ava—even if I'm not so sure he's my Link anymore.

And that's assuming he ever *was*...

The next night, Link is home by ten. Knowing that that means he'll be gone as soon as I fall asleep, I wait for him to come to bed before *I* initiate this time.

I have before. It took me a few nights to get used to his appetite, and for it to trigger something in my own. The way I saw it, if he expected my duty as his wife was to be available to sleep with him whenever he wanted me to, I might as well get as much pleasure out of his rugged, brawler's body as I can.

I do that night. Instead of laying back on the pillows, letting Link worship me with his mouth like he loves to do, I take a firm grasp on his erection, steering him right where I want him. As soon as I have him there, I smile to see the hungry look on his face, the way his tongue darts out, licking his bottom lip as he rises up on his elbows, watching as I crawl between his legs.

And then, taking a page of his book, I show him how much he's mine with actions instead of words.

Link loves to watch me suck his dick. He always has. For as long as we've been intimate, he's never treated the act like it was something he owed. To him, me going to my knees in front of him reminds him of dropping to his knees in front of the pew during Sunday Mass, only instead of listening to the priests talk about all the reasons why we're both going to hell, he mutters prayers under his breath as I take him to Heaven with my tongue and my teeth.

I've caught him stroking the rosary inked on his forearm sometimes while I tease him, squeezing the base of his shaft while swirling my tongue around the circumcised head of his penis. Then, when calling for Mother Mary doesn't give him any relief from me, he would jab his nails in his skin, fucking my mouth, trying to hold out as long as he thinks I want him to.

Tonight, I'm not torturing him, even though—in the heat of the moment—Link insists he still deserves to suffer. That he'll be serving his penance until the day he fucking dies... which, now that I have him back, better be when he's ninety and too weak to hold a gun, but still strong enough to shove his wrinkled dick inside of me while I'm snoring.

Tonight, I worship the man who saved me, even while sentencing me to a life with him.

He thinks I'm being punished. Having a gorgeous gangster obsessed with me, a penthouse to protect me, and the luxury to pretend I never pulled a trigger and took a life... if this is Hell, I'm happy to burn.

From the way Link pants as I hollow my cheeks, taking him deep while his prayers tonight are a repeated chant of *my wife, my wife, my fucking wife* over and over again as he slowly begins to rock his hips, nearly gagging me on his thick dick... from the way he throws his hands behinds his head, letting me take control of his big body... from the way he tries to pull out moments before he shoots his load, but I graze him with my teeth, warning him to stay right where he is as his salty spun fills my mouth...

My husband is right there with me.

Once I swallow and he catches his breath again, Link hooks his hands under my armpits, dragging me up the length of his naked body. I know exactly what his plan is. He's going to finger me, playing with my pussy while he recovers from his own orgasm. Sometimes he prefers to keep tugging until I'm sitting on his face, where he takes his leisurely time licking me before he's hard again and I'm suddenly riding his dick.

If there's one thing I can say about Link—and why I was so taken aback that time in the bathroom—it's that he's always been a generous lover. He got to come. He won't leave until I get to, too.

But I didn't suck him off because I wanted him to reciprocate. Tonight, I wanted to enjoy my husband —and fool myself into believing that he really is mine.

"Just hold me tonight," I whisper. I lay my head on his chest. "I want to hear your heart beat."

One arm wrapping around my shoulders, he tangles his fingers in my hair. "You should," he rumbles, the vibrations tickling my cheek. "You're the reason it fucking beats at all."

I wish I could believe that. "Mmm."

"What? You think I'm full of shit, Ava?"

No. I think he's saying what he thinks his wife wants to hear.

When I don't answer him, he gives a gentle tug on my hair. "I don't lie. Not to you, Ava. Never to you. You have to know that."

Only... I don't.

And that's not all.

I want to ask him what we're doing. What *he's* doing. In this room—in this *bed*—I know that he's as much mine as I'm his... but what happens when he inevitably leaves it in an hour or two to return to his business?

I don't, though. It would only be a waste of breath. Because Link? He means it when he says he won't lie to me. He never has.

But that doesn't mean he always tells me the truth.

So I stay quiet, my head leaning against his right pec, my finger tracing the cross that covers his left side, following the twists and curves of the script dashed right over his heart while I still have him here with me.

If someone handed me a pen and told me to close my eyes, then slipped a sheet of paper in front of me before telling me to draw this particular tattoo of his, I could do it. That's how much it's imprinted on me in the time since I've got to enjoy Link's naked body.

It's a reminder that I so often need. Scrawled in the middle of the cross, written in an elegant script as though it's the most important thing in his world, are two words: *the life*. Despite the different designs he has inked all over his body, they're the only written tattoos, and it's clear to me what it means.

It's a tribute to being in organized crime, and Link's way to show anyone who might see his cross that he's devoted to being the head Sinner.

They come first, and I have to remember that.

the life

Mrs. Crewes

TWENTY
LOUISE'S FLORALS

AVA

My admittedly impressive blow job skills buy me two days with Link returning to the overbearing, overprotective, neanderthal of a husband that he was shortly after our marriage.

But then, as I hoped it wouldn't, things go right back to the way they were. Link, finding any excuse to leave the penthouse. Me, wondering how I'm going to spend the rest of my life as his pretty little trophy wife, tucked out of sight until he decides to get serious about that heir of his.

Instead of spending time with me, he really amps up the gifts. It's like he's trying to use material things to make up for his distance. After the third package is handed off to me by one of him men, I finally tell Link over dinner that it's too much.

Of course, his only answer is, "I've worked hard to be able to spoil my wife," and I feel like a bitch for trying to stop him.

I don't need to be spoiled, though. Even when we were two stupid eighteen-year-olds, playing house in a dump of an apartment, he would promise me that, one day, he'd have enough money to buy me whatever I wanted. He never understood that all I wanted was *him*.

Those days, when I had to bandage Link up after another brawl in the back alleys that brought in just enough for groceries for the week, I was happy if he found a flower for me in the concrete jungle we lived in.

Feeling vulnerable one night, I remind him of that. It's not about the money. It's about the thought. The effort.

The affection.

No surprise that he shuts down the conversation, using his masterful touch and claiming kiss to distract me from feeling like we're miles apart, even when we were sitting on the same couch together. And whether he understood what I was trying to say or not, the packages stopped.

The flowers didn't.

Every day, like clockwork, an elaborate bouquet arrives for me. There's always a single card, written in a delicate script that has to belong to the florist. It says, *To my wife* and it's signed *Lincoln*, with the florist's logo —a place called Louise's Florals in downtown Springfield—stamped on the bottom.

It's a different bouquet every time. They each come with a glass vase, overflowing with every single type of flower you can think of... but there's always one that looks like it's been plucked from the local park. Whether it's a dandelion or a different wildflower, it's tucked inside, and though I know it has to be an order he gave to the florist, I can't help but get butterflies in my belly whenever I find it.

I keep them. I keep all the flowers, with Mona beaming whenever I ask her to find a home for the latest vase, but the wildflowers? They're special to me, and I keep them pressed between the pages of the first edition copy of *Little Women* Link bought for me.

Because of small things like that, I can look past a lot of things that Link does, blaming it on his position in the syndicate.

The late hours. How he seems to spend more time in meetings at the Devil's Playground than with me. The way he insists on my having a bodyguard in the penthouse—and at least three when I want to step foot outside of it.

And then there's the fact that he has two phones: a recent model, and a smartphone that looks like it's a couple of years old. I only ever see him using the updated phone—and while his conversations around me are often short and in code, they're still super frequent—but he keeps that second phone charged and ready at all times.

I brought it up once. As his wife, I was expected to hand my phone over to his tech guy so that he could put some apps on it. A tracker, Link admits without an ounce of shame, and one that would prevent someone from breaking into it if I ever lost it.

He doesn't go through my messages—though there haven't been many since I got whisked away to his world, and most of my teacher friends are too busy on summer break to know that my life has changed so drastically—so I can't bring myself to go through his, but I'd be lying if I said I was dying to know what the purpose behind having two phones was.

All I get out of Link is that one's for business, and one's personal. I can't imagine how—as far as I can tell, he doesn't *have* a personal life apart from our stolen moments in the penthouse—and that tracks since I never see him use that phone.

He keeps it on him anyway, and I let it go.

I let a lot of things go... until I discover a second card tucked in my afternoon bouquet while searching for the wildflower hidden inside.

I know I shouldn't have opened it. It came in an envelope addressed to Lincoln

"Just a note that we've started the process on your second arrangement, as requested."

Blinking rapidly a few times, I make sure I read that right.

Second arrangement.

Who else is Link sending flowers to?

With the note from the florist in my pocket, I wait until Bobby hitches up his pants and heads for the bathroom to make my escape.

Bobby is my usual afternoon babysitter; after it all got out that the shaggy-haired Kyle had a bit of a crush on me, Link threatened his nuts if he acted on it, then banished him from the penthouse. I guess, since he's in a committed relationship with Heidi, Bobby was safe enough to have around me, so he's usually there.

One good thing about having the same guards over and over again? It's easy to pick up on their routine. Around this time every day, Bobby takes a twenty-minute shit in the bathroom assigned to the men.

With Mona working on dinner prep, I grab my phone, my license, and my debit card, and slip into the elevator.

After that night at the Playground, Link insisted that I don't leave without telling him. That way he can arrange for me to have a couple of bodyguards if he's too busy to accompany me wherever I want to go. I never *said* I would do it; I just did it as a courtesy to my husband and his position.

But since I know damn well that Link would stop me, I decide it's worth a little risk. I won't be gone for long, and though I could've just called Louise's and asked about the second arrangement, my gut tells me that this is a conversation I want to have in person.

The florist probably won't tell me anything. With as much money as Link has got to be dropping with them, keeping me in roses, peonies, daisies, and more, it's a pretty safe bet he'll have her loyalty. But, you never know. Maybe Louise will take pity on one of her customer's wives and give something away when I'm actually standing there on the other side of the counter.

My phone starts ringing when I'm halfway across town, riding in the Uber I hired. I had it on my lap, a safety measure in case my driver was sketchy, and I notice him looking at me funny when it instantly starts to ring again once it stopped the first time.

Sparing a smile and a half-shrug, I glance at the unfamiliar number—it's not Link's, or anyone else I know—and slide it under my jeans to muffle the vibration.

After six calls, it finally stops. I pay my driver, thanking him and declining his offer to stick around. Something about him made me uneasy, and I'd rather walk home than climb back in his car.

I wait for him to leave me on the side of Main, just outside of Louise's Florals. As soon as he disappears back into city traffic, I slip my phone into the back pocket of my jeans and glance up at the shop.

It's cute. Its sign looks hand-painted, with the name of it drawn in a pretty sky-blue script over a soft pink background. It's a bright spot in the dingier part of Springfield, and I find myself smiling a little as I push open the door, a gentle *ting* announcing my entrance.

A curvy brunette is standing behind the counter, head bowed over some kind of ledger. She has a pencil in her hand, tapping it absently against the countertop, humming under her breath as she tucks a strand of her long, way brown hair behind her ear.

As she hears the *ting*, she glances up, revealing a lovely face and warm hazel eyes. "Hey, there. How are you? What can I do for you?"

Apart from the coolers full of flowers, the counter and its old-fashioned register, me and the woman, the shop is empty. Fingers crossed that she's the owner, then, since I don't see any other employees.

"Hi," I say. "I'm actually looking for Louise."

The brunette purses her lip, an apologetic look flashing across her face. "I'm sorry, but she's not here. She's actually on a well-deserved vacation for the next week."

Damn it. "Oh."

She folds her hand, the massive engagement ring and matching wedding band on her left hand clinking against the glass countertop with the motion. "I'm

Angela. I manage the shop when Louise isn't around. Maybe there's something I can help you with?"

Maybe. I pull out the crumpled card I stowed in my front pocket. "I had a question about this."

I have a question about who the hell else my husband is sending flowers to.

As though subtly showing off her rings—and making me almost want to flash the tattoo on my finger right back at her—she stretches out her left hand, waggling her fingers.

I press the card into her palm.

Angela takes it, running her gaze over the message. And then, to my surprise, she grins.

"Ah. So you're the lucky lady."

"What?"

"Mrs. Crewes, right? Lincoln's wife."

I nod. "I found this in the bouquet that arrived for me this morning."

"Well, that was a mistake. The runner who picked up the bouquet today was supposed to hand that off to the housekeeper."

My stomach goes tight. Mona knew, too?

It finally dawns on Angela that while she's happily chatting away, my world is falling apart. Not only is Link setting up a second floral arrangement for God knows who, but Mona has been helping him hide it from me.

She tilts her head, hair falling over her shoulder. "You know, I mentioned it to my husband. When we were planning our wedding, he knew better than to think about having any input when it came to the flowers. I'm somewhat of a hobby botanist, you know, and I had connections with Louise. He handled food, and I did flowers. I couldn't understand a bride who didn't want to have a say in her own floral arrangements."

Um... what?

"Floral arrangements?" I echo.

"Right. That's what the note was about. He had very explicit instructions about what kind of arrangements you two were going to have at your wedding in September."

What wedding, I wonder. Because, as far as I know, we already had our quickie wedding back at Judge Callihan's.

Angela realizes that I have no idea what she's talking about a few seconds later. Gasping softly, wincing, she covers her mouth with her hand. "Whoops. I forgot. Lincoln said it was a surprise."

"A surprise?" I echo weakly. "What do you mean, surprise?"

She shakes her head. "I shouldn't have said anything."

Probably not, but now that she has... "What exactly did my husband say?"

I can see the war playing out on her features. Does she piss off the Devil of Springfield—or piss off his wife, and have to deal with him anyway?

"He might've mentioned something to my husband

about giving you the big church wedding you missed out on by eloping. I guess, since me and Mace eloped, too, doing the courthouse thing, he wanted some advice on hosting a second wedding before God or something like that. He said it's been taking up all his time, but it was worth it for his wife."

Oh.

Oh.

Honestly, that is something we talked about. Not recently, but years ago. Even though we were "living in sin" at eighteen, Link was adamant that we'd get a priest to marry us when we finally said 'I do'. Being the silly little girl I was, I wanted the poofy white dress, the pomp and circumstance—

—and the *flowers.*

Oh...

the life

Mrs. Crewes

TWENTY-ONE
MY WIFE

AVA

I thought he forgot about that the night he chose a civil ceremony for us. I should've known better. It wasn't like he could force a priest to marry us with a half an hour's notice—not like he did with the judge—but when he never brought up having a second ceremony, I didn't either.

Is this... is this what he's been doing behind my back? Not cheating on me, but doing whatever he could to give me the wedding of my childhood dreams.

I don't know what to say. Stunned by what Angela told me, I lift my fingers to my lips, tapping them with the tips, trying to make sense of all this.

Because... it makes sense, right? Or do I just *want* it to?

"I like your ink."

I glance over at her. Not gonna lie, but I wasn't expecting the compliment on the heels of what she just said—especially when I'm not sure which one she's referring to.

Taking pity on me, Angela taps her knuckle. "Your tattoo. It actually gives me an idea that my husband might like. He's actually a bit of an artist himself." A secretive smile tugs on her lips. "I have a few tattoos he gave me already."

They must be hidden beneath her clothes. She's wearing a silky blouse and a long flowing skirt, but unlike my devil tattoo and Link's name on my finger, none of hers are on display.

Before I can say anything in response to that, her eyes light up.

Hurrying around the countertop, she says, "Speak of the devil," a moment before the door opens.

For a split second, she says 'devil' and I expect Link to come stalking through the door.

Nope.

It's a *cop*.

Dressed in an SPD uniform, the man walks with the energy that he owns the place. He's not as big as Link is, though I'll admit he fills out his uniform very nicely. He has carelessly tousled black hair, steely blue eyes, and a smile curving his lips as he sees Angela running toward him.

He opens his arms up to her, lifting her off the ground, spinning her around before setting her back on her feet. Pressing a kiss to the top of her head, he releases her, then says, "I missed you, angel."

She giggles. "I've only been at work for four hours, Mace. And you stopped by when I opened."

"I know. I still missed you." He turns to look at me, a quick up and down before dismissing me just as easily. "Busy?"

"All morning, yeah. It's a good thing Louise let me come back to help her, and so she can finally take a break. Summer's definitely our busy season."

The cop—who, from her reaction and the thick gold band on his ring finger, must be her husband—loops his arm over her shoulder in a possessive manner. Squeezing her to him, nuzzling her close, he says, "I can't wait for it to be over. You and me, we'll take an extended honeymoon." Another kiss, as though he can't help himself, and then, "You know how much I like it when it's just the two of us, angel."

I envy them. They're obviously still in the newlywed stage, with the way he can't keep his hands to himself, and how she looks up at him with big doe eyes as she says, "I do."

And then there's me, who never got a honeymoon, but if Angela can be believed, it's because Link's planning another wedding for us first...

"I just wanted to stop in while I was patrolling this way," her husband tells her, though he makes no move to release her. "I didn't mean to interrupt you if you're with a customer."

Angela pats him in the chest. "Do you know who this is, baby? It's Mrs. Crewes. Lincoln's wife."

Before, he gave me a quick once-over, scrutinizing me with those dark blue cop eyes, and dismissing me just as fast. But now... I don't like the way he's looking at me now.

Almost instinctively, my eyes dart to his nameplate.

M. Burns.

Crap.

Just my luck.

"I have to go. My husband... I should get back so that I can meet him in time for dinner."

It's not a lie. He'll be back at the penthouse soon enough, and then we're going to have a talk about just what he thinks he's doing.

I remember how, a few times when he thought I was already asleep, he murmured how he wished we could start over. Depending on his mood, I couldn't decide if he meant he wanted to when he left me—or how our second chance began with him blackmailing me.

Maybe it did. Our lives got derailed that day, but maybe we were always meant to find our way back to each other somehow. Link, the bigshot gangster. Me, the naive school teacher. As we are now, we probably should never work as a couple... but he married me. If he has it his way, and Angela's not covering for him, then he'll do it again.

Still watching me closely, Burns nods at me. "Do me a favor, yeah?"

"Um. Sure."

"Let Devil know me and my angel will be at the wedding, would you? Consider it our RSVP."

There goes any kind of secrecy. Angela might've let it slip, but there's no way she tipped her husband off to back up her story. It has to be true... and I really hope that I'm not just being hopelessly delusional.

"I will."

He nods, and I get the feeling that he's dismissed me.

Good.

With a wave at Angela, I turn on my heel, heading right for the door. I'm already thinking about how I'm going to get back to the penthouse because I know—I just *know*—that Burns is going to call Link up and let him know that he ran into me at the floral shop.

I'd planned on walking before, at least far enough to avoid being assigned the same creepy Uber driver from earlier. I wasn't in Louise's long enough for him to be out of the local area, and I didn't mind the idea of getting some exercise while it was still light out.

Knowing that I just ran into Officer Burns? That dashes that idea. I need to get back to the penthouse ASAP so that I don't cause Link an aneurysm by worrying about me.

Just as I step out onto the sidewalk, ready to grab

my phone and order a car, I hear someone call my name.

My head snaps up in time to see Bobby hopping out of his car, dancing around the cars whizzing past him as he jogs over to me.

Wow. I mean, I know Link made it so that I can be tracked if necessary, but I guess it never occurred to me that one of my bodyguards would be able to find me. It probably should have. If they're responsible for me while Link is occupied, they'd have to be able to track me down.

And Bobby? He did.

Breathing through his nose, the heights of his cheeks red with either panic or annoyance, he storms right over to me.

"You didn't answer the phone," he says, raising his voice at me. No 'hi', no 'hello', no 'how are you'... just a very accurate accusation. "What the hell. Do you even have it on you?"

Not that I need to prove anything to him, but I take it out, showing it to Bobby. "If Link wanted to call me, he could've."

He didn't. I have eight missed calls currently, all from the same number. Bobby's obviously.

"That's because he has no idea you left on your own. And we're going to try and keep it that way, okay?"

"He'll understand." When I explain that I let my jealousy get the better of me... if there's anyone in the world who'll understand my motives, it's my husband.

Bobby snorts. "Trust me. It doesn't matter who you are, you don't want to piss off Devil."

I'm not so sure about that.

Link will be annoyed, but he won't be angry. Not at me. But Bobby, on the other hand... this is the second time he let me slip away. No wonder he's freaking out. If the Devil comes out to play because his wife went missing, it's Bobby's head on the chopping block.

That's why I don't struggle when he grabs my bicep, dragging me toward the car that he double-parked. He's probably desperate to get me back to the penthouse before Link realizes I left it.

I let him. He has a car, he can obviously cross the town quick as hell since he made it hear so soon after I did, and we both want me to get back before Link finds out where I went.

Bobby throws open the passenger side door for me. Just as he's shoving me roughly inside of it, I feel a pinch that catches my attention, and has me yelping, "Ouch."

He pauses. "You say something?"

"Yeah." He finishes manhandling me into the car, and I go even as I tell him, "Something pinched me."

"I know."

He *knows*.

Before I can ask him what that means, he makes sure I'm completely seated, then slams the door closed.

By the time he's made it around the back of the car, sliding into the driver's seat, I'm already feeling... *off*.

My vision is going dark. My tongue feels too big in my mouth, and it comes out as a slur as I ask him, "What did you just do to me?"

The last thing I remember is the triumphant smile tugging on his thin lips as Bobby shows off the small needle nestled in his palm.

After that, everything goes black.

LINCOLN

If wedding planning isn't one of the seven circles of Hell, it should be.

I thought navigating a three-way stand-off between local mafias when it comes to gun running was rough. That's nothing compared to figuring out how much food to order from the caterers, or whether Ava would prefer a morning wedding or one in the afternoon.

I eventually book St. Francis's for an eleven o'clock ceremony because that would give her time to get ready before I drive her over to the church. A Sinner's reception usually goes all night, but my wife likes to turn in early. This way she doesn't get shafted by cutting the party short, and I get the chance to show her again just how important she is to me in front of the Family.

Because kid or no kid, the moment I made Ava mine, she made the syndicate a Family. We don't need a fancy church wedding to prove it—the scene at the Playground was more than enough—but I'm not doing all of this because it's expected of me as the head of a crime family. If I was, I would've delegated all of this to one of my soldiers or even Ava herself and washed my hands of it.

Oh, no. I'm doing this *for* Ava, giving her the wedding she always dreamed of, and hoping like hell that she finally understands that she's my wife.

I fucked up. I admit that. Marrying her the way I did... I'll never regret making her mine, but by doing it as fast as I did, I didn't think about what she wanted.

Now I am, and I hope she appreciates it when I'm done.

A small smile curves my lips as I think of all the ways Ava will show me that she does on the honeymoon I'm also planning—

My phone buzzes, cutting short my imaginings.

"Fuck."

Again? I just got off the phone with the caterers, and if they're calling back with more bullshit questions like "chicken or steak" again, I might blow my top.

Snatching my phone, I barely glance at the name on my screen—but then I do a double-take and answer it. "Burns? You got an update about Maglione for me?"

On the other end of the line, Burns sounds quieter than I'm used to. Deadlier. "You'll never guess who I just ran into."

If he's telling me, there's a reason he thinks I care. "Who?"

"Your wife."

I nearly drop my fucking phone.

I'm in the back office of the Playground, dealing with all of this wedding shit. Because it's a surprise, I can't do any of it in front of Ava, so I've been spending most of my time here, calling it 'work'.

If Burns showed up at Paradise Suites, someone would've called me. Mona. Bobby. Even Ava… someone would've called me. Then again, it should've been the same thing if Ava left.

What the hell is going on?

"Where did you see her?"

"Funny thing, Devil. She was leaving my wife's shop as I was walking in."

Burns's new wife works as a florist at the place where I've been ordering all of my flowers for Ava. As a favor to him and for all of his help, I thought I'd throw a little business Angela's way. Ava likes flowers—and she loves the little additions I throw in—but that doesn't explain why she would risk leaving the penthouse without telling me just to go smell some roses.

"Hang on," I tell the cop. With Burns still on the line, I pull up the tracker app Tanner installed for me. When the address where Ava's phone is at appears on my screen, I recognize it instantly. "She's still there. Can you do me a favor and put her on the phone?"

"I watched her leave, but maybe she's waiting outside for a ride. I'll go check."

I hear the jingle of a bell, a door opening, the handcuffs on his belt jangling… and then, "I don't see her."

What the fuck does he mean, *I don't see her*. "My app says she's there."

"Right, and my eyes say she isn't."

Asshole. Burns is the best cop on my payroll in the SPD, but he's a fucking asshole. Hitting a button on my app, I signal it so that Ava's phone will start ringing. It's supposed to be used when she misplaced her phone in the penthouse, but this will work, too.

"I just made it ring," I tell him. "Do your ears work?"

"Funny, Crewes," mutters Burns. "Real fucking funny—hey. Wait a sec. I think I do. It's coming from—*oh*."

Oh? I don't like 'oh'.

As if he can read my mind, Burns breathes out, "You're not gonna like this."

"Where is my wife, Burns?"

"I think I found her phone." Static as Burns shifts his. "It's an iphone, blue case with apples all over it?"

Yeah, because she was a teacher. "Yeah. Where did you find it?"

And why isn't Ava on the line yet?

I get the answer to that when Burns says, "In the street, just on the other side of a parked car. It's here. She's not."

Each word echoes like a bullet to my brain.

In. *Boom.* The. *Boom.* Street. *Boom.*

It's. *Boom.* Here. *Boom.*

She's. *Boom.*

Not.

Boom.

I squeeze my phone so tightly, the glass enclosure creaks.

"Where the fuck is my wife?"

Burns doesn't know.

And neither do I.

the life

Mrs. Crewes

TWENTY-TWO
DAMIEN

AVA

I come to with a scream. Eyes clamped shut, feeling as though I've been ripped out of a nightmare, I scream and I have no idea why I am.

My head feels fuzzy. My body aches. Wherever I am—whatever happened to me—I'm lying down on something lumpy, my hands trapped in front of me. I can't move them, and the realization that I can't has me screaming louder.

Until I hear someone snap at me and I jam my jaw shut in terror that, whatever's going on, I'm not alone.

Someone scoffs, and I screw my eyes even tighter. It's as though, if I can't see it, the trouble's not there, and oh my God, what is going *on*?

"Shh. There's no need for that." My head feels fuzzy, but I know that voice. I can't quite place it yet, but I *know* it. "Come on, Ava. Stop with this princess crap. They might treat you like that on the West Side, but the East End is different."

East End? What am I doing on the East End?

The last thing I remember, I was in downtown Springfield. I was at the flower shop and then... and then—

Bobby.

My eyes spring open, and Heidi Fox—former third-grade teacher at my school and current waitress at the Devil's Playground—is standing over me, a look of annoyance on her face. She's not wearing half as much make-up today as the last time we met, and while she's not in the same uniform, her current outfit would definitely fit in as one of the clubbers.

Glancing down, avoiding the way she rolls her eyes as I start to panic, I see that I'm stretched out on a couch. My hands are cuffed together in front of me. I don't know where this room is, but apart from Heidi, a small table, and the couch, it's empty. No windows, either, and the only door is positioned directly behind Heidi.

If I could even flop off of the couch with my woozy body and my cuffed hands, I'd still have to get past her to leave, and something tells me that Heidi's standing next to the couch to prevent exactly that from happening.

Bobby drugged me, I remember. With whatever was in the vial he injected me with, he drugged me and

THE DEVIL'S BARGAIN

I have no idea how long I was out for, why he did it in the first place, and where I am now.

"What's going on?" I ask Heidi. "Where's Bobby? He... he shot me with something, I don't know why, but I'm... where am I? Why do I have cuffs on?" I rattle them, the metal biting into my skin. "I want them off. Can you help me get them off?"

As if in answer to each of my questions, Heidi simply shows me her forearm—and, at the very least, I know the answer to that last one.

Can she help me get them off? Probably, but Heidi's not going to, is she? And the fresh tattoo on her skin explains exactly why not.

The last time I saw her at the Playground, she had the red devil horns inked on her skin, like everyone else who works for the Sinners Syndicate. Not anymore. A dragonfly with teal and green wings is covering up Link's mark.

A *dragonfly*.

At the beginning of the summer, I had no idea what that would mean. Since entering the life as Link's bride, I've had a crash course in all things organized crime. From the hierarchy in each family to the unspoken rules they all follow... and what each brand means.

Link's is a devil.

The dragonfly is the mark of the Libellula Family.

Trying not to show how freaking out I am that I'm in cuffs, lost, and staring at a woman who's wearing the brand of the man whose soldier I shot a month and a half ago.

Keeping my tone light, I say, "I thought you worked for Devil?"

For *Link*?

Heidi raises her eyebrows. "You mean your husband?"

She knows. I'm not surprised that she does since Link introduced me to the Sinners—and she's Bobby's girlfriend—but the way she says it? It's almost a sneer, like I did something wrong by being Link's wife.

Welp. If she's wearing a Libellula tattoo, I probably did.

"The Libellula Family are my husband's rivals," I say, not even trying to deny my relationship to Link. "It's one thing for you to trade loyalty from the Sinners to another syndicate." I think. I'm not so sure about that part. "I'm assuming Bobby did, too. But why bring me here?"

Heidi looks slightly uncomfortable. "Don't blame, Bobby, okay? He did this for me."

"I don't understand."

"He was never going to rise up the ranks as a Sinner." She scowls now, and there's no doubt it's meant for me. "They had him on babysitting duty, for God's sake. If I want to get out of teaching, we need money. Both of us. He wasn't going to get it with the Sinners. But Damien..." The way she whispers his name is so reverential, I want to throw up. "He'll take

THE DEVIL'S BARGAIN

care of us. And all it cost was finally getting you away from Devil and taking you to him instead."

The urge to puke is even stronger now, and not only from the effects of whatever Bobby drugged me with. I did this. My jealousy and my need to prove to Link that a relationship can't be built only on "ownership"... I did this.

How much do you want to bet that Bobby would've sold me out to my husband's enemy long before now if I gave him the chance?

I thought he was being friendly. That I was being sneaky. *Idiot*, Ava. He didn't just tell me about Link's frequent trips to the Playground out of the kindness of his heart. Especially since, when I arrived there that first night, Link wasn't *even there*. Heidi was, though, and I have no idea what would have happened to me if Link didn't show up when he did.

He was smart. He insisted on bodyguards when I left the penthouse, and what did I do? Sneak out again —while Bobby was on duty—only to be relieved when I saw that the soldier had chased me down because it meant I didn't have to rely on a rideshare.

Oh, no. I just served myself up on a silver platter for him. Now I'm on the East End, at the mercy of Damien Libellula, and no way to contact Link.

Something tells me, even if I somehow find a way to get these cuffs off, it won't matter. My phone's probably long gone, and so is any chance of getting out of here.

No. I refuse to believe that. There has to be a way—and I get to believe that for about two seconds before the door behind Heidi pulls outward, replaced by a slender man in a black suit.

His skin is a deep tan, his thick hair as black as coal with a single grey streak along the curve from his left-side part. His eyes, however, are a pale blue that seem even lighter compared to his dark coloring.

He's a handsome man, and he carries himself like he absolutely knows it. I'd put him at about forty or so, with a countenance of a man who demands results. Like a CEO or a... a...

"Mr. Libellula," Heidi breathes out when she sees him standing there.

Crime boss.

"Ms. Fox," he says, tilting his head in her direction. "How's our guest?"

"I did what you told me to. I sent the text when she woke up and kept her calm until she got here. Can me and Bobby go now?"

The man flicks his fingers at her. "I'll have Vin contact him if I need you again."

"Yessir." Heidi bows her head, backing away and out of the room. "Of course. Thank you."

"Close the door, would you?"

As soon as she does and it's just the two of us, it's like she was never here. He doesn't just demand results. He commands attention, and I can't help but give it.

Looking down at me, he *tsks* his tongue. "Cuffs, really? For an unconscious woman who couldn't hurt a fly." He pauses for a moment. "Unless, of course, she has a gun."

Holy shit. Holy *shit*.

He *knows*.

Giving me a smile that makes his heartbreakingly stunning, he crouches down so that he's at my side. "But since we both know you don't, I see no reason why she should be trussed up like this."

Dipping his hand in his pocket, careful to keep his jacket closed though I can't help but notice the bulge at his hip telling me that *he* does have a gun, he pulls out a tiny key. Within seconds, he pops off one cuff, then the other. Taking them away from me, he shifts and tosses them on the empty table with a *clang*, then slips the key back into his pocket before rising up to his full height again.

"That's better," he says. "Isn't it?"

I rub my wrists, but stay quiet.

"Very well. Maybe we should get introductions out of the way. You, of course, are Ava Crewes, née Monroe. But do you know who I am?"

I do, but I can't bring myself to say his name out loud.

Taking that to mean that I'm clueless, he shoves up the sleeve of his suit jacket. Unbuttoning the white shirt underneath, he rolls it to his elbow, revealing a tattoo.

It's a massive dragonfly. At least six times bigger than Heidi's, the wings wrap around his deceptively muscular forearm, in shades of blues, purples, and greens.

"You see this?" he purrs. "It isn't just my calling card. It represents my family."

Not *the* family. *My* family.

And that's why I know exactly who this is: Damien Libellula, in the flesh.

The same man that sent Joey after me and started this whole thing all those weeks ago when I shot him...

I don't think that's why I'm here. From his sly comment before, it's obvious that Damien knows that I'm responsible for what happened to Joey. Not just responsible, either. I mean, I *killed* him. But if this was just about revenge for that, would he really have gone through all this trouble?

Or does this have everything to do with the man who's been protecting me ever since?

"You must be wondering why you're here," he says, so conversationally, you'd almost think he wasn't a notorious gangster. "The answer is very simple. I didn't take you. Devil gave you to me. A peace offering, as it were, between our two families."

See now, *that*? That finally gets me to find my voice.

Pulling myself into a sitting position so that I could look up at him with scorn, I tell him, "You're lying."

"And why would you say that?"

"Because he loves me.

It might be in his own way, and that's on me for disregarding every time he's whispered it while we were together in bed because *I* wasn't ready to reciprocate, but he loves me.

And even if he didn't? I belong to him, and he will never, ever let me forget that. Whether I belong in his world or not, if there's one thing I know for sure, it's that he would never go through the trouble of marrying me... of moving me into his penthouse... or claiming me in front of the Sinners Syndicate only to pass me off to another man.

The man is planning a wedding behind my back because he probably thinks being doubly married means I'll finally admit we've had a legit marriage all along... no way he just tossed me to the side like Damien wants me to believe.

Instead of pushing his lie, he says, "How well do you know Devil?"

"I've known him nearly my entire life."

This time, Damien tuts. "I didn't ask you how well you know Lincoln Crewes. I asked you how well do you know *Devil*." He pauses for a beat. "Do you even know how he earned the name?"

I don't answer him because, honestly, I can't. It took years before I realized that the Devil of Springfield and my Link were one and the same, and by then, I purposely avoided hearing any of the lurid rumors people were spreading about him.

That's all right. In his cultured voice, watching me

closely for my reaction, he tells me explicitly how Link became the Devil of Springfield.

He probably meant to shock me. In a way, he does.

I had no idea that Link got the name because of *me*.

When he's done, there's only one thing I can ask: "How do you know? I mean, how can I know that you didn't just make all that up? You already lied once before."

"That's true. And when you see Lincoln again, you can ask him all about it. But how do I know? Very simple. We worked for the same guys those days long before we branched out on our own." Another very effective pause before he adds, "We were friends."

"And now you're enemies."

"We don't have to be," Damien says pleasantly.

What?

"You were right. Smart girl that you are... you're not here because Devil gave you to me. You're here because I need a meeting with your husband and you, Saint Ava, are the leverage I need to get him here."

Saint Ava.

He says it just the way Joey did before he died, but just like then, I have no idea how Damien knows my old nickname.

Ignoring the way he said he needed me for leverage, I focus on the name.

"I hadn't had contact with Link in years when you sent Joey after me. Taking me hostage then wouldn't have done anything."

A dark look flashes over his refined face. "I didn't send that idiot anywhere. He was newly inducted into the Family when he first heard the whispers of Saint Ava. He put two and two together on his own, and thought he would throw you at me to get back at Devil. It was a relief when I heard through the grapevine what happened to him."

Is it? Oh, thank God.

He nods at the sigh of relief I can't keep back. "Exactly. I want loyal soldiers who do what they're told, not idiots who think for themselves." He huffs. "And, honestly, if there's anyone to blame, it's your husband. He was the one who put out word through the streets that Ava... *his* Ava was untouchable. Good guys got a pass, but the rest of us... we all knew that he was watching you from the shadows, making sure everyone treated you right. Maglione did... until he fucked up after he got his dragonfly. Even with shit for brains, it didn't take long for him to realize his ex-girlfriend and Devil's Madonna were the same."

Most of what Damien said is like an angry buzz in the back of my woozy mind. Most of it, except for the part about Link.

My mouth goes dry. I try to swallow to get some moisture, but it doesn't work.

Untouchable? Link made me untouchable? He watched me?

He never forgot about me at all?

What?

"Don't you wonder where you got the name from, dear? For as long as I've known him, Devil has worshiped you. And that is precisely why you're the leverage I need."

I ignored him before when it came to that.

This time, I don't.

"Leverage?" I repeat. "Leverage for what?"

He doesn't answer me. He doesn't get the chance.

All of a sudden, the door inches open. I almost expect it to be Heidi again, but it isn't. Instead, a young man wearing a suit a little too small for him tiptoes into the room.

Damien quirks an eyebrow. "Yes?"

"We just got the call. It's a green. Sixty, boss."

"Ah." Damien brushes the younger man off, sending him scurrying back out of the room. Then, shifting his suit jacket, pulling out the gun I knew was there, he smiles at me before dropping his gaze, checking to see how many rounds are in it. "Time to go, Mrs. Crewes."

He must have understood something in that coded message that I didn't.

"Go?" I echo. "Where?"

"It seems as if your husband has agreed to my terms. We don't want to leave him waiting, do we?"

Oh, no.

Link.

the life

Mrs. Crewes

TWENTY-THREE
DEAL WITH THE DEVIL

LINCOLN

If you asked me this morning, I would have said the most significant phone call in my entire life was when I was sitting at the Playground and saw Ava's digits pop up on the screen.

It's still up there, but the call I got from Burns about fifteen minutes ago tops it.

I always knew that the crooked cops of the Springfield PD double-dipped. For the right price, anyone could buy Mason Burns especially. Like me, he only has loyalty to one person—his wife, Angela—and he treats the rest of the world as disposable.

Even so, we have a good enough working relationship that I'm not surprised Damien Libellula got wind of it. Why else would he have picked Burns to pass his message along to me?

Damien wouldn't call himself. That's not his style. He has a tendency to delegate in a way that I never got the hang of, and what made us good partners before we split up and each started our own crime ring.

In the beginning, we worked a lot of jobs together. But fifteen years is a long time, and money does strange things to people. The Sinners Syndicate took over our turf on the West Side, the Libellula Family claimed the East End, and so long as we stayed apart, we could coexist.

Of course, then Royce was blamed when a Dragonfly's sister was killed, and friendly rivals turned into enemies in the middle of a turf war.

Royce wasn't responsible. I put the whole syndicate on the line to prove that, but the damage was done. I haven't talked to Damien in six years, and I've done everything I could to keep us apart.

Until now.

Until he used one of my guys against me to steal my *wife*.

The message made that clear. Damien Libellula has Ava on his turf, but he's willing to give her back if I meet with him in an hour's time on neutral territory. He assured Burns that she was perfectly safe and sound and would stay that way so long as I agreed to the meet.

Then, to show that he had good intentions, he gave Burns the name of the Sinner who sold me out, willing to abduct Ava and carry her off to the East End of

Springfield for a thousand bucks and the promise that he could become a Dragonfly.

Robert Cullens, better known as Bobby—and the Sinner I trusted to watch over my wife before she disappeared earlier this afternoon.

I should've known better, but now that I do, I'm going to take care of it.

I have to meet Damien Libellula in—I check my phone—forty-three minutes. With Luca behind the wheel, I can make it to the meeting point in fifteen, maybe ten.

If Royce did what I asked him, too, I'll have more than enough time to make the meet and take care of some business.

I ENTER THE PLAYGROUND THROUGH THE BACK, MOVING at a quick clip to reach one of the empty offices set along the same stretch of hallway as the conference room. When I see Royce leaning up against the door, his back to it, ankles crossed in front of him, some of the red dimming my vision fades a little.

The promise of revenge does a lot to help a bastard like me see a little clearer.

My second nods at me. "All set, boss. Just like you thought. Dumbasses were celebrating at the Playground, acting like they didn't do anything wrong."

"They?"

"Yup. I got Bobby and his girl in the room, as requested."

My lips curve into a wicked grin. That's exactly what I wanted to hear. "Thanks."

"You want me to stick around?"

I glance at my phone again. I haven't put it down since Burns's first call almost eight hours ago, and even after his second, the edge of the device is a furrow against my palm. No way in fucking hell will I miss a single ring if I get an update on my wife.

I'm down to thirty-two minutes. I gotta make this quick. "Yeah. I'll need clean-up."

"Rolls" Royce is the best gambler in the syndicate, my trusted second, and a pretty damn good fixer. Of all his skills, though, I put him on clean-up duty because he likes it, and if that's another way he deals with his demons, who am I to judge?

"I'll be waiting."

I clap him on the shoulder, then reach for the doorknob.

Inside the office, Bobby is standing with his arms crossed, eyes darting toward the entryway when I fill out. I can see the sweat beading on his brow from across the room and know instantly how this is going to go.

His girl—Heidi Fox, thirty-three, and formerly a waitress at the Playground until she abruptly quit four nights ago—is sitting in a chair, one leg crossed over the other. The top one is bouncing. Her nails are tapping the tabletop, though she doesn't look at me as I stride into the room, tugging the door closed behind me.

Nervous. Both of them are nervous.

Good.

I don't have time to ease them into telling me what I want to know. They'll lie, they'll deny it, they'll try to tell me I get it wrong... and I'm on a deadline here. I'm not dealing with that bullshit.

I point at Bobby. "You. Roll up your sleeve. Show me your mark."

"Devil—"

"I didn't ask for any commentary. I said roll up your sleeve. So roll up your fucking sleeve, okay? Now."

He gulps, Adam's apple bobbing as he pushes his long-sleeve shirt up.

The newly inked dragonfly is all the proof I need to know that he's in this up to his eyeballs.

I don't care why. I don't give a shit that he's a Dragonfly now. The Sinners aren't for life. He could've walked away at any time and I could've replaced him easily. The only thing I demand is loyalty so long as you wear my brand, and he's not wearing it, is he?

But he fucked up when he touched my wife.

Something must have passed across my face because Bobby's hand jerks a second before he covers the tat up with his sleeve.

I'll give him credit for having balls when, instead of dropping to his knees and begging for my mercy, he juts out his chin and says, "You mad that I changed sides?"

"Nah."

I took the wind out of his sails with that one, didn't I?

"Oh. Okay. I mean, no hard feelings, right? It's just... I got a better opportunity with Damien's crew. You know how it is."

He's right. I do.

And that's why I check my phone again—thirty minutes to go until the meet—and, slipping it in the inner pocket of my suit jacket, I trade it for my gun.

"This isn't about the Sinners, Bobby. You tried to take away the most important thing in the world to me. You saw what happened to Twig. You had to know that I wouldn't let that go."

His eyes go wide and wild. "A pussy? You're pulling a gun on me for some snatch? Devil, man, *c'mon*."

Is that all he thought she was?

Ava talked about him with me. She liked him, and when I got pissed he let her slip away to the Playground, she asked me not to punish him. It's for the same reason I didn't hold it against him when Ava disappeared today. He was at the penthouse, supposedly taking a shit when she left it, and he was still there when Glenn came to relieve him before Burns called to tell me he saw her.

He was fast. He must've had a window of about a half an hour to pass her over to Damien's Family without arousing suspicions, and he might have gotten away with it if Damien himself didn't give him up.

But he did, and I'm down to twenty-nine minutes.

"You take from me," I tell him, "I take from you."

Bobby stiffens. Heidi whimpers, but she's still purposely avoiding the death in my eyes. It's not going to save her. I'm too far gone to be merciful. This is Skittery all over again, and if I had time, I'd really make it *hurt*.

Too bad I don't.

I lift the gun.

Bobby gulps. "Are you... are you really going to hurt my girl, Devil?"

"She's just a pussy, isn't she?"

I watch as it hits him. I swear to God, we gotta do a better job vetting these new Sinners. Look at this one. He's another dumb fuck. To him, my *wife*'s only worth was in her body. But threaten *his* woman? And he's suddenly realizing how serious I am.

I look at my Sig and sigh. "I don't think I can avoid it."

And then I shoot him. Once in the skull, once in the chest, once in the cock.

He was dead at the first bullet. The other two just make me feel a little better about finishing him off so quickly.

Falling out of her seat, crawling on her knees over to where Bobby is crumpled on the floor by the wall,

Heidi lets out a shriek that might've moved me if I wasn't obsessing over my Ava screaming just like that.

Royce pokes his head into the room. "All done, boss?"

I jerk my thumb at the wailing woman. "Take care of the traitor and the collateral damage, would you?"

"You can trust me."

I know I can. That's why I have no problem leaving Royce to clean up another mess.

Me?

I'm going to get my wife.

Thanks to my driver, I make it to the meet with three minutes to spare.

I'm not surprised that Damien picked this part of town. This particular alleyway, either. It's dark, especially closing in on midnight, and none of the locals will look twice down it. Even if they do, they'll look away again, and no one will involve the cops.

I know that for a fact. After all, this was the exact spot, fifteen years ago, where I lost control when Skittery threatened Ava.

Damien knows, too. He wasn't there that night, but he was the one that our old boss assigned to help me clean up the old junkie's remains.

For the next two years, we were as tight as thieves,

each one working toward something. I wanted Ava. Damien wanted his Family.

Now, fifteen years later as I walk into the alley to find him standing at the back of it, holding Ava at gunpoint in front of him, I realize that we both got what we wanted for a short amount of time. I had my wife if only for a few short weeks. Damien had the Libellula Family for more than a decade—but unless he can do what he promised Burns he would and explain himself to me, one of us is going to lose what we hold dear the most tonight.

And it's not fucking gonna be me.

"So glad you found us, Lincoln," he calls out. He has his gun in hand. So do I... and if Ava wasn't positioned as a shield between us, I would've taken my shot and ended this without having to do this at all. "I wondered if you could find the place. If you remembered."

To Ava and Royce, I'm Link. To the rest of Springfield, I'm Devil.

But to my old friend, I've always been Lincoln.

"Yeah. I remember." When he quirks his eyebrows at me, I shrug. "Skittery."

Ava's eyes widen in recognition at the name. They shouldn't... but they do.

How?

"Forgive me," Damien says. "I told the story to your wife earlier. I guess she didn't believe it could be true."

Of course not. Even when presented with evidence to the contrary, Ava has only ever seen the good in me.

I needed her to. That's why I forbid any one of my men from telling her anything I've ever done as Devil, starting with the murder that kept me away from her for so long. I never wanted her to know what I was capable of. For fifteen years, I strived to be a better man... and maybe I'm not.

Maybe I *am* Devil. Heidi Fox would definitely agree that I am. And while I did my time, I did my *penance*, I protected Ava as best I could, I've decided that the only way to keep her safe was with me. Even then, I fucked up. She wouldn't be standing with a gun at her back if it wasn't for me, and I decide then and there that it doesn't matter.

I'll save her, but I'm not giving her up.

"You got me here, Damien. Just like you wanted. Burns passed your message along. If I showed up to talk, you'd give me my wife back. Drop the gun. Let her go."

I didn't honestly believe that would work. When we were partners, Damien's best quality was his sense of honor. I'd lie to anyone and everyone—except for Ava, of course—but Damien? He thought it beneath him.

Oh, no. He preferred to manipulate and maneuver people instead, like they were pawns on a chessboard.

Then again, I haven't had anything to do with him in years. Maybe he changed—because I'm definitely caught flatfooted when he crooks his arm around

Ava's waist before I can react, tugging her against him. The mouth of his gun kisses her temple, an obvious threat.

If I make any sudden move, he'll kill her. No hard feelings, just a casualty of the war brewing between his family and my empire. To Damien, she's just a bargaining chip.

To me, my wife is *everything*.

"You asshole," I rumble. "You said you'd let her go."

"And I will, Lincoln. But I also told Burns she was my leverage. This talk is a long time coming, and I'm not going to let her go until we... negotiate."

Negotiate? "Negotiate *what*?"

"Territory. Terms." In the moonlight, his pale blue eyes seem to flash. "A truce."

This is why he had Bobby take my wife? Because he still has this ridiculous idea that, with a truce, he could move drugs into the West Side, and I can expand my operations into the East End?

"You've gotta be fucking kidding me."

"I'm not."

He better be. "You really think you can call me out here, in the shadows of Springfield, threaten my wife after *kidnapping* her, making me wait eight fucking hours to find out you had her... and I'm just going to shake your hand, make a truce, and not hack your head off like I did Skittery?"

For some reason, Damien takes my very reasonable—and absolutely serious—threat as a joke. He doesn't laugh, though the moonlight reveals his tiny smile as he nudges Ava with his gun.

I growl, but neither one of them reacts... until he says to Ava, "I don't know, Mrs. Crewes. Do I?"

Ava?

She licks her lips, eyes turned pleasing. "Link, please... listen to him."

"Ava..."

Her name is like a prayer on my lips. She doesn't sound frightened—though any civilian with a gun to their head *should*—and I found out why when she calls out, "He just wants to talk. He said... he said that, if you agree to a truce, I'm covered. He won't come after me for what happened to Joey. I don't have to worry about it anymore, but only if you agree. Please... I think this would be good for us."

Us...

If I agree, there is no 'us'.

Okay. I finally get it. Damien has wanted a truce for as long as we've been rivals, and his efforts only increased after what happened with Royce and Heather. I shut him down every single time because I couldn't see how it benefited me.

Now I do. He's using my wife, just like he said. She's leverage for him to get what he wants.

And because I'm a sorry sap, I'll do it because Ava just begged me to.

"Deal," I spit out. "You got your fucking truce, Damien. You know my word is good." When it comes to something like this, it has to be otherwise I would never command any respect as the head of a syndicate. To go back on my word… that would be the same as giving him the green light to eradicate the Sinners and take over our territory. "Ava's my witness. Royce will listen to her. You're set."

"What about you, Lincoln?"

That's pretty simple. Damien gets what he wants. Ava gets what she wants.

And since I'm the one who lost, there's only one thing that makes sense in my cold, lonely mind.

From the moment I became the Devil, I discovered how easy it was to solve all of my problems with death. Skittery threatened Ava? I went cold and massacred him. Twig thought I'd let her touch him willingly? Dead. Bobby betrayed my wife? Blown away.

I'm about to lose Ava again?

"You don't need my protection anymore," I tell her, and I jerk my hand, digging my Sig Sauer into the flesh beneath my chin.

She gasps, and Damien curses under his breath.

I keep my hand where it is.

"Link? What are you… put that gun down!"

I don't. "I only got to keep you because you needed me to keep the cops coming after you. I did. Then you needed protection from the Libellula Family. I thought I could use that to keep you at my side… but if he's not gunning for you, what reason do you have to stay?"

"What reason?" Her lovely green eyes glitter with

angry tears, pushing against Damien's arm as though she's forgotten about the gun to her head. "How about because I love you, you asshole?"

I stumble back on my heels. "What did you say?"

"I love you, Link. I love you, I love you, I love you... and if you blow your head off and I don't get the chance to tell you, I'll figure out a way to bring you back from the dead and kill you myself!"

My lips kick up in a small grin, heart pounding harder than it ever has.

That's my spitfire.

My Ava.

My *wife*.

I lower the gun at the same time that Damien simply releases her. It has to be that. He's not as strong as I am, but he could've kept Ava right where he wanted... but he drops his gun to his side, letting her run to me.

If I wanted to, I have a direct shot at him. If he wanted me dead, he could turn his gun on me. So long as Ava isn't being threatened anymore, I could give a shit what he does.

Only I do.

Because she *loves* me.

That realization makes me feel fucking bulletproof. Damien can fire every round in his gun. I don't care. Ava loves me.

I throw open my arms as she launches herself at

me. Lifting her off the ground, I squeeze her to my chest as she buries her face in my neck.

Even then, she can't stop telling me how much she cares about me.

"I married you because I needed it. I was scared. Terrified. I didn't want to go to jail. I had no idea why any of the mobsters in the city would be after me... but if you'd walked back into my life at any point in the last fifteen years, it wouldn't have mattered. I was meant to be your wife. I love you, you big idiot, and I can't wait for "

"You know?" I murmur.

"I know," is all she says before the tears finally begin to fall, sobs following shortly after, the heat of her tears scalding me beneath the collar of my shirt.

Over her head, I meet Damien's icy blue eyes. His hands are empty, I notice, as though he's already honoring this truce he wants between our factions.

It won't last. I have no idea why Damien thinks this is the right time to work together, to combine our might, and move our specialties into each other's territory. Back when I knew him, I could never figure out how his mind worked; I was always the brawn to his brains, just like Ava is my beauty.

"You agreed to the truce," he reminds me.

"I did."

He taps his pocket. "You shoot me now, or pull a Skittery on me, my men will know. You won't like how they avenge me."

I'm sure I won't.

Damien always was a smart fucker. While the only backup I have is Luca, Damien must have a radio or something to connect him to one of his men. That way, he didn't break the spirit of our agreement—that we would both enter the alley alone—but I can't break my word when there are other witnesses than just my wife.

My *wife*.

As if reading my mind—and sometimes I wondered if he *could*—Damien points at Ava.

"Do a better job of protecting her," he tells me. "If I could get her that easily, someone else could, too."

Someone else? When we're the only two players in Springfield? If I'm protecting Ava, and so is Damien, who else is there to worry about?

I go to ask him, but he's already gone. Disappearing down the far end of the alley, slipping off into the night, the Dragonfly flies away—and I know that that's not the last I'll see of him.

the life

Mrs. Crewes

EPILOGUE

AVA

So relieved to be back with Link, I thought he might take pity on my ordeal and let me go to sleep before he starts to interrogate me about what happened.

Yeah... I was wrong.

He doesn't instruct Luca to head right home. As though desperate to just keep me in the sanctuary of the back seat of his blacked-out ride, he has me straddled over him, my arms wrapped around his neck.

It just felt natural to assume this position. Once he gave Luca the order to keep on driving until he's ready to stop, Link lifted me on his lap. For the first few blocks, I was curled up against him, just enjoying the feel of his hard body beneath me, his heart beating against my boobs, but then I realized just how hard he was.

Reaching down, I stroke Link through his pants. Next thing I know, I'm lifting my ass off of him, helping him ease my jeans down past my ass. He groans when he sees that I didn't wear panties today—that I'm ready for him, just the way he likes—and as he throws his head back, I work his zipper down.

There's no need to undress him entirely. While I'm naked from the waist down, I only need his cock to be free. The second it is, I sink down on top of him, keeping him warm. Then, flicking the first few buttons on his shirt open, I lay my cheek against his chest for a moment, enjoying the feel of his skin against mine.

With his dick inside of me, keeping that connection and sending shivers of pleasure through me whenever Luca "accidentally" hits a pothole, Link strokes my neck possessively as he listens to me tell him everything that happened today.

I make a mistake. I start at my arrival at Louise's Florals, take him through meeting Angela and Officer Burns, and how I ran into Bobby when I was planning on calling an Uber before he drugged me, then ushered me in the car.

After I get a quick lecture that I should always, *always* call Luca if I need a ride, no matter what—that he echoes from the front seat because, yeah, he's totally listening in our conversation—he spurs me to continue.

THE DEVIL'S BARGAIN

I can't. Not yet.

"Are you mad at him?" I ask as Link switches to running his knuckle over the curve of my shoulder. The rest of him is still, as though he wants to keep from any movement that might make him come before we make it back to the house. "Bobby, I mean."

Because he obviously knows the part that my old babysitter played in putting me right in Damien's hands. True, I really was only leverage to get Link to agree to this truce of theirs and I never was in any real danger—especially since he removed all the rounds in his gun before he grabbed me, something that I'm not sure I'll ever admit to Link—but the leader of the Libellula Family gave me a few more details on our ride over from the East End to the alley.

To get Link to agree to come, he told him that he had me, and that the reason he did was because of Bobby. At the time, I wasn't so sure how Link would react, and... yeah. That's a total lie.

I watched him shoot Twig. I heard the story of how he got his name.

That's why I'm not even a little surprised by his answer.

"Bobby's dead," Link says flatly. "I spared the girl. I didn't kill Damien. But Bobby's dead."

I leave it at that, continuing with my story because it's exactly what I expected to hear. When I get to the point when I woke up to Heidi hovering over me, he mutters that he should've shot her, too, while he had the chance.

I'm kind of glad he didn't. I mean, if I see her again, I'll claw her fucking eyes out for her part in leading Link to think his only move was to put a gun beneath his chin, but she didn't deserve to die for listening to the man she loved.

After that, I explain in more detail how Damien convinced me that a truce with the Sinners would help out my husband, and then spend the next five minutes chewing Link out for the stunt he pulled with his gun.

In between pressing kisses to my throat, my big brawler of a husband apologizes for the first time in our married life. He apologizes for scaring me, and for me being put into the position I was, all because I was his wife.

Of course, I cut him off right there. I told him in the alley how I was meant for him, and that wasn't just a plea to get him to stop with the foolishness with his gun. Seeing him ready to end it at the idea that I might not be his wife any longer made me stop hiding behind the idea that it didn't matter *who* he was married to.

But it did, and my jealousy turned into a possessiveness of my own. He's mine, and if getting abducted by suave mobsters comes with the territory, *fine*. Next time, I'll just make sure not to sneak out without a bodyguard…

Only one problem. Link's not concerned about *next* time.

He wants to know about *this* time.

And when I don't immediately admit to the reason why I left the penthouse in the first place, he lays his hands on my hips, ready to lift me off of his dick.

I don't want to go anywhere, and to stop him in his tracks, I blurt out, "I was jealous, okay?"

He slams me back down on top of him. "Jealous? Of fucking what? I told you, Ava... you're the only one I've ever wanted. Everything I've done... everything I *do*... it's for you. I'm the one who's jealous of any man who gets to look at your smile for the first time. Who gets to experience your laugh for the first time. Who gets to see the vision that is your ass from behind before I threaten to gouge out his eyes for looking at you... but what can you possibly be jealous of?"

When he puts it like that, it sounds so ridiculous. Link told me he would never lie to me, and I never doubted him. Why would I think that he'd suddenly want a mistress?

But I did, and burying my face in his thick throat again so he doesn't see how embarrassed I am, I own it.

I thought he'd chuckle. If not that, maybe scoff.

Instead, he slips his hand between our bodies, lifting me up by the chin so that I'm forced to look into his dark eyes.

"Ava..."

I huff. He's not going to stop until he gets me to admit everything, is he? "You can't blame me. I find this card that made it seem like you were buying flowers for two women—"

"Because of the floral arrangements for the wedding. Yeah. I know. Burns told me."

Right. "That's why I went down to the flower shop. 'Cause I was irrational and I was jealous and I thought they might give me an address for your mistress or something..."

His lips curve. "And what would you have done if they did?"

Honestly? If I got my hands on a gun, I might have shot her. And why not? I already killed someone once. Maybe it gets easier the second time, right?

I don't tell Link that, though. I don't have to. As if he can see the answer written on my face, he tugs my chin toward him, kissing me.

I'm breathless when he's done, and delusional if I thought he was going to drop the subject.

"Was that it?" he asks.

I want to say yes. But, in the back of his car, driving circles around Springfield, I realize that I might as well get everything out in the open.

"You have two phones," I tell Link. "I know you're not into drugs since that's Damien's thing, and the only people I can think of who have two phones are drug dealers and cheaters."

I don't know how Link's going to react to me calling him a cheater in a roundabout way, but it's definitely not with a low chuckle as he shifts his hips.

THE DEVIL'S BARGAIN

I gasp, enjoying the sensations as his dick goes just a little deeper, falling forward, bracing my hands on his hips as he reaches into one pocket of his pants, then the next. Like always, he's carrying both of them, and he tosses the phones on the seat next to us.

"Go on. Call it."

What? Even if I had my pants within reach... "I don't have a phone."

Reaching into his pocket again, this time he pulls out mine.

"Where did you get this?" When I checked my pockets earlier, I didn't have it. Damien didn't, either, and I thought I must have dropped it if Bobby didn't do something to it.

"Burns found it on the side of the street," he tells me. "It's how we got a head start knowing something was off." Nodding at the phone, he adds, "Don't distract me, Ava. Call my number."

I do.

As soon as I finish dialing Link's number, his personal phone rings.

"Okay. So it works."

He nods, then passes over his business phone. "Call it with this one."

I still don't see where he's going with this. But, he seems insistent that I do this, and it's the least I can do after what I put him through just now because of my jealousy.

I dial his number and... nothing happens.

Weird.

I do it again, but after I press the last digit, I hear a tiny *click*. Like it's being disconnected.

I glance up at him. "You block your own number?"

Link shakes his head. "I block *every* number. Every number, that is, except yours."

"What?"

"Tanner... he's our tech guy... he made it so that no other numbers can get through. I keep it charged every day. I always have."

I still don't understand. "Why would you do that?"

"I've held onto this phone every day for fifteen fucking years, Ava. Willing it to ring. Hoping it would. Then, when it finally did, I took it as a sign that my penance was done. You would finally be mine, and if I had to sin again to keep you, I would. Because I'm a Sinner—"

Dropping my phone somewhere behind me, I nip at his lip, swallowing the moan that replaces what he was going to say next when I kiss him. Pulling away, smiling down at him, I say, "You're not just a Sinner, baby. You're my husband."

"And you're mine," he rumbles, rolling his hips up, making me ride him like he's my favorite roller coaster.

As I come down from it, my eyes land on the tattoo on his chest that I revealed when I opened the top part of his shirt.

"You know... now that we're being all honest and open with each other—"

He drops his hand, flicking my clit with a devilish smirk. "I definitely have you open right now, my wife."

I shudder out a breath. He's the one who told me not to distract him before, and what is Link doing now? The same thing to me.

Point. I had a point.

What was it?

Ah.

"It's something else I've been thinking about lately. About how I have your mark on me," I remind him. "Two actually. So, tell me, husband: when are you going to have Cross put me on you? Or is that going to be after our second wedding?"

I thought he'd take my tease as light-hearted as I mean it. If anything, he has an excuse to tell me about the wedding he's kept secret from me for all these weeks.

But he doesn't.

Instead, he blinks, almost stunned. "Don't you know?"

"Know what?"

Link taps his chest, using his pointer finger to underline the scripted *the life* drawn over the center of the cross on his left side.

"Ava, love, you were the reason for the first tat I ever got."

"Huh?" I was.

"I couldn't risk writing your name on my heart. Heading the syndicate... I built it up so that, one day, I could use it to protect you. But until I could, I never wanted anyone else to come after my heart. Writing 'Ava' over my heart might've put you at risk. So, instead, I wrote this."

He pats the scripted part of his tattoo again.

"I looked up what your name meant on the internet," he admits, almost shyly. Thirty-five, a hardened killer, and he's almost blushing in the interior light of his fancy car "Had to go to the library to do it, but the website I found said Ava meant 'the life'. And that's what you are: my life. You always have been, even when I wasn't a part of yours."

But he is now, all because I called his personal line and he came to rescue me. Then, when he did, he took the opportunity to blackmail me into becoming his wife.

Which I did. It was a deal with the Devil, but I definitely came out on top.

And, as I wrap my arms around his neck again, pressing my lips to the tattoo over his heart as his stiff cock stays buried to the hilt inside of me, I mean that literally.

LINCOLN
THE DEVIL

The Devil' Bargain

AVA
THE BRIDE

AUTHOR'S NOTE

Thanks for reading *The Devil's Bargain*!

I hope you enjoyed reading about Ava and Lincoln's second chance romance. If so, please make sure you sign up for my newsletter for a bonus short story set at the end of this book featuring these two!

Also, if you purchase a physical copy of this book—paperback, discreet paperback, or hardcover—send me your mailing address via email (carinhartbooks@gmail.com) and I'll mail you a free bookmark and a signed bookplate!

This is also the beginning of a series that will feature both the Sinners Syndicate and—eventually—the Libellula Family. The next one will have "Rolls" Royce as the hero, and if you like how possessive Link is over his Ava, wait until you see what happens when Royce wins a night with Nicolette.

Also if you're interested in learning more about

AUTHOR'S NOTE

Officer Burns and his new wife, their book is already out now: No One Has To Know. It's a stalker/captive romance, and proof that the cops in Springfield are just as bit a danger as any of the gangsters.

Thanks again, and keep reading for a look at Royce and Nicolette's book (available for pre-order now), as well as a sneak peek at the opening to Burns and Angela's story!

xoxo,
Carin

PRE-ORDER NOW
IT WAS SUPPOSED TO BE FOR ONE NIGHT ONLY...

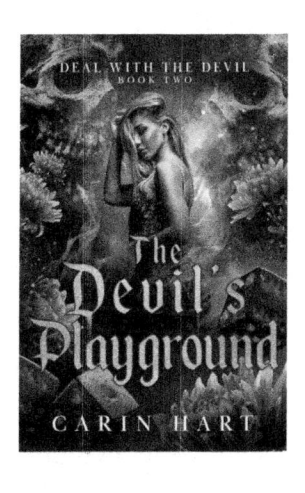

In the Devil's Playground, a Sinner always plays to win.

NICOLETTE

I needed money, and I needed it *fast*.

When my job as a hostess at the local Italian place wasn't going to earn me enough to cut it, I did the one thing I promised I would never do: I got involved with one of the syndicates that rule Springfield.

Considering I'm trying to avoid anyone with ties to the Libellula Family, I head to the West Side, and hope like hell the Sinners Syndicate will give me a chance.

The Devil's Playground isn't my first choice, but

what else can I do? I make it clear that I'm only interested in serving drinks... until some big shot gambler offers me ten grand for one night.

I take him up on it—only to have wager his night with me to another guy... and *lose*.

Now I'm expected to honor my deal with the Syndicate's underboss, and the charming bastard who hired me for this job in the first place.

ROYCE

From the moment Nicolette walked into the Playground, I wanted her—but then I brought her on as one of our girls, and she was suddenly off-limits.

I learned the hard way: work and pleasure don't mix. If I'd met her anywhere else, I might've taken a shot at the waitress, but she needed the job more than she needed a boyfriend, so I backed off.

And, okay, that's a damn lie. I didn't pursue her, but hell if I didn't take a page out of Devil's book and start watching over Nic from the shadows...

I would have left it at that, though, until one of the Playground's more well-known wallets set his eyes on my girl.

They don't call me "Rolls" for nothing. I played him for the night she agreed to, telling myself that I was just saving her from what the sick and twisted customer wanted to do to her.

Then I get my first taste of Nicolette, and I realize

PRE-ORDER NOW

that one night will never be enough... and I'll stop anyone who tries to take her from me.

The Devil's Playground is the second book in the **Deal with the Devil** series, a collection of interconnected standalones set in the fictional crime hotspot of Springfield. It tells the story of "Rolls" Royce and the one woman he'll do anything to save, Nicolette Williams.

Releasing January 27, 2024!

NO ONE HAS TO KNOW

A SNEAK PEEK AT OFFICER MASON BURNS AND HIS ANGEL...

MACE

It's all the fucking daisy's fault.

Not like I need something to blame for my obsession. I don't. I know what I am, and I accept that I would've locked on my angel with or without the flower eventually. Something put her in my path, the perfect prey to my predator. The daisy just sealed the deal.

I'm a bad man. I do what I want—take what I want—and the whole damn world lets me because I have a badge.

It's the perfect disguise, too. As much as cops get shit on, there's a reason so many of us turn out to be garbage. Something about the job calls to a certain type of twisted soul, and I answered the call when I realized it gave me a cover to the darkness inside of me.

People see the uniform first. The gun next. Sometimes the cuffs, or the badge. Rarely do they pay attention to the man instead of the symbol, and that's exactly how I like it.

I'm the one who gets to watch. To observe.

To judge.

Angela Havers thinks I'm a good guy. The friendly cop that patrols outside of Louise's Florals, the small florist shop in the middle of my beat. You wouldn't think flowers would be a big draw in the middle of such a rough-and-tumble neighborhood on the edge of Springfield. You'd be wrong. People seem to appreciate the spot of brightness in the middle of a concrete jungle.

Me? I only give a shit about my pretty little florist.

Seven years my junior, she has an innocence about her that makes her seem even younger. At least until you get a good look at her lovely hazel eyes and realize that they're haunted.

She's seen some shit, but it didn't break her. She's still my angel. Sweet and tender and so utterly delicious, she makes my mouth water for a taste that I can't have unless I want to devour her whole.

She's kind, too. As a cop, I'm used to getting comped. Freebies are part and parcel of having the badge, especially when half the territory you're patrolling is full of criminals, the other made up of the good folk who like the facade that we're here to protect them.

NO ONE HAS TO KNOW

Maybe my fellow cops are. Me? From the moment she shyly flagged me down months ago, offering me a single daisy to brighten my day, I've only ever cared about keeping one soul safe. Of watching her, of learning all her secrets, of obsessing over the moment I could find a way to make her mine.

My angel.

At the very least, she needs the protection. Her innocence blinds her to just how dangerous Springfield can be. I know that all too well. Lowlife crooks scatter around the city like cockroaches, looking up to gang leaders like the dark figure who conducts his business out of the aptly named Devil's Playground.

Meanwhile, Devil himself thinks he rules the streets as easily as he controls his club, his runners, his girls, and his business—and for a favor here and there, and a weekly deposit into my checking account, that's perfectly fine with me.

So long as none of his men set their eyes on my woman.

I let it be known that she's under my protection. Anyone who even looks twice knows what's coming for them, and while Lincoln Crewes might be known as the Devil of Springfield, the brawling gangster at least has *some* morals.

I have fucking *none*.

Which is why, after slipping into her apartment building one afternoon months ago, going up to her floor on the pretense that I was answering a fictitious call, I was pleased to see that she had a decent deadbolt lock on it. I'd slit the throat of anyone who thought to hurt my angel, but that wouldn't mean anything if I lost her before I could make her mine.

But while she's got the deadbolt covered, what was the point when she doesn't bother shutting up her windows? It's like a fucking invitation to the worst of us, cop or criminal. Anyone with bad intentions could sneak up the fire escape and let themselves into the sanctuary of her bedroom.

Which is why I spend nearly every night I can climbing into her apartment, standing guard over her as she sleeps.

I find peace in her snuffling snores, and rage in her frequent nightmares.

She's been hurt. My innocent flower has scars she carries deep that only come out when she's sleeping. Her whimpers have me reaching for my gun every goddamn time.

I don't have a name. Can't get one, either, without showing my hand. So, forcing myself calm no matter what it takes, I vow that, if any bastard tries to hurt her again, I'll be there to show him what true justice looks like.

And if I ever get the name of the prick who already did?

He'll live to regret it.

Oh, wait. He *won't*.

I never stay in her shabby studio apartment for

long. A few hours—when the worst of the worthless crooks in Springfield are up to no good, and Devil and his goons run the night—before I begrudgingly head back to my empty bed across town; it's not my home, but a place I put my head down between patrols. I have a hunting cabin—my *real* home—up in the hills for when the city life turns me feral and I need some peace before I go rabid, but I haven't gone back since the daisy wilted and died, and I started to worry that the same thing might happen to my precious angel.

The cabin is just too far from her. What would I do if she needed me and I was an hour away? Hell no. I have to keep close because, given how sweet and innocent yet broken she is deep down, the wrong sort of man is attracted to a woman like her.

Ask me how I fucking know.

AVAILABLE NOW

IT WAS SUPPOSED TO BE FOR ONE NIGHT ONLY...

HE LOVES ME, HE LOVES ME NOT...

ANGELA

I love flowers. Being a botanist has always been my dream, but life got in the way—and, nowadays, I have a job at the flower shop near my crummy apartment. So that's something, right? Maybe it's not in the best neighborhood, but it's a bright spot in a dirty city, and at least there are usually cops around.

I've noticed one in particular lately, keeping an eye on the shop. Officer Mason Burns. I'm friendly enough

—though I can't bring myself to trust anyone in a uniform after what happened to me a couple of years ago—and that ends up working in my favor when I'm attacked for the shop's deposit one night.

Burns comes to my rescue, arresting the would-be robber with the knife, and I'm super grateful for his help.

I'm a lot less grateful when I end up in handcuffs the next time we meet... or when he brings me home with him to be his prisoner.

BURNS

On the surface, I'm a hero—but that's the surface. The truth is that I'm a bad man. A possessive man with my own sense of right and wrong, and of justice. I've never pretended to be anything else, either. I do what I want... take what I want... and they let me because I have a badge.

I also have handcuffs and a gun, but they're not my only weapons. When it comes to Angela Havers, my best one is a deceptively charming smile.

She thought I was going to save her. That's where she was wrong. My obsession with the sweet little florist might have saved me—but it will be her undoing.

Unless she gives in to me, body and soul. Because my angel is mine...

...and no one has to know.

AVAILABLE NOW

*This is a dark romance—including stalking and captivity—and is written for adults. It has mature themes and language, and a hero who thinks he knows exactly what the heroine wants... and if she doesn't, she eventually will. There is also a HEA, though I do recommend readers check the 'look inside' for the foreword before committing to reading.

KEEP IN TOUCH

Stay tuned for what's coming up next! Follow me at any of these places—or sign up for my newsletter—for news, promotions, upcoming releases, and more:

CarinHart.com
Carin's Newsletter
Carin's Signed Book Store

facebook.com/carinhartbooks
amazon.com/author/carinhart
instagram.com/carinhartbooks

ALSO BY CARIN HART

Deal with the Devil series

No One Has To Know *standalone

The Devil's Bargain

The Devil's Playground

Dragonfly

Dance with the Devil

Ride with the Devil

Printed in Great Britain
by Amazon